FROZEN

◆

CARLA TOMASO

Copyright © 2012 Carla Tomaso
All rights reserved.

ISBN: 0615657680
ISBN 13: 9780615657684

ALSO BY

CARLA TOMASO

Voyages Out—a collection of stories published by Seal Press. "...the writer immerses readers in psychological drama. All of Tomaso's narrators take great emotional risks. Highly original characters." (Publishers' Weekly)

The House of Real Love—a novel published by Penguin/Plume. "...funny, very funny yet also passionate, searching and serious...sex and the dance of intimacy fill this book with the immediacy they give to life." (Los Angeles Times)

Matricide—(Penguin/Plume) "The book is funny, moving and horrifying. The narrator's bravado and cynicism are tempered by bursts of romanticism, creating tension that reveals her vulnerability and humanity." (Publishers' Weekly)

Maryfield Academy—(Haworth Press) "A fast, furious, and very funny dash across the plains of healthy bad taste. The book is rich with scenes where the text wanders off into weird yet wonderful observations." (The Gay City News)

FOR MARY

ONE

◆

As I got closer to my mother's hospital room I said my secret prayer.

Let her be dead.

I knew perfectly well she'd be alive. Earlier that morning her devoted caregiver, Doreen, had called me to say she was in again for a skin infection on her leg. Not good news but not death either.

So here I was carrying a box of chocolates and ten pounds of old photos in a Trader Joe's sack. A therapist had recently urged me to orchestrate the big breakthrough with Mom, which, she assured me, would significantly improve my own personal life, romantic and otherwise. According to the shrink, something only Mom could fix was wrong with me, and time, evidently, was running out. Although she wasn't dying today, the doctor said her heart wasn't going to last the year.

I wanted her to die and at the same time I was frantic to get her to love me.

It wasn't going to be easy. She had never liked me, even when I was a cute kid.

As usual when I visited, I peeked into patients' rooms as I went by. The healthier ones were chatting and looking at cards and flowers with visitors, laughing even. Everybody else was asleep and dying, in that sad fetal position most of us come back to, full circle, at the end.

Mom's regular room had the best view in St. James Hospital, overlooking Newport Harbor with those multimillion-dollar homes and gray/pink sunsets. Beyond that, on a clear day, was the outline of Catalina, where Mom and Dad used to spend drunken weekends with their boating friends and sometimes me.

She couldn't see any of it now unless somebody helped her over to the window. But it wasn't important to look at the view. Just knowing it was there, behind the bed and to the right, cardiac care unit, room 1308, was enough for her.

When I walked into her room the bed was empty.

"Mom," I said. My heart jumped. Was she dead after all?

Nope. She was crouched on all fours peering underneath the hospital bed. Doreen was bent beside her in much the same position except that my mother was almost naked, her sagging breasts touching the dappled gray linoleum floor. I was reminded of the chapter about the Houyhnhnms in *Gulliver's Travels*, where the humans are the degraded animals and the horses the exalted aristocrats.

Although she'd always indulged her appetites like a greedy child, my mother was no dumb animal, at least not usually. She was a wealthy old woman with bad knees, weak lungs and a worn out heart. She ate dessert instead of salad and popped Percodan whenever anything hurt.

"Helen, scoot backwards and I'll fix your nightie," Doreen said. "Elizabeth is here."

Doreen was a fit and attractive woman, which was a good thing because my mother couldn't handle the fat or ugly and had to be helped up a lot. And although Doreen was foreign, Polish, at least she was white and smart. It went without saying that Mom was uncomfortable with people of color and hated the stupid even more than the ugly.

"I want to visit the Tahitian village under the bed," she shouted at Doreen.

"Mom," I said again, putting down my bag. "Can I help? I brought you some chocolate."

"She must have snuck in some of her own meds," Doreen said. "I was using the bathroom and she slipped out of bed."

"Who the hell are you, fat woman?" Mom said to me as we pulled her up and tried to tie her hospital gown so it wouldn't fall off again. "Are you a nurse?"

"I'm Elizabeth," I said. "Your only child."

And I wasn't that fat. Most people I was close to, including my ex-girlfriend Min, thought that I was big-boned and well proportioned.

"There is no Tahitian village, is there?" Mom continued.

"Nope," I said. "You're whacked."

"Help me to the bathroom then."

I waved Doreen off. She'd been up all night bringing Mom to the hospital and getting her settled. She was dead on her feet. Luckily, Mom didn't notice or she would have demanded that Doreen stay. Even while hallucinating on pain meds she was the most selfish woman in the world.

I watched as she sat down on the toilet, the pastel gown opening again and falling gently to the floor. My mother's body was layered, latticed with scars, most of which were new to me. I hadn't seen her naked in awhile. Her legs were marked with wounds that took weeks to heal. There was one on her right calf now, covered with gauze and that angry-looking infection simmering darkly on her thigh. Between her large breasts was the long pink scar from open-heart surgery, and on the left side of her knee, the scar from the replacement last year.

Old and wrecked as it was, I admired her body for functioning in spite of her enormous neglect.

"Get some toilet paper," she barked. "Wipe me."

I did.

They're trying to take my money," she whispered as I put her back in bed. "It's in my shoe."

I ignored that and went to work, handing her the first photo from my bag, a black and white of her holding an infant me as far away from her body as her arms would reach.

"You were such a smelly baby," she said. She dropped the picture and pinched her nose.

At least she seemed to be sobering up. She knew who I was.

I handed her a second photo, a small child at the beach standing with a bucket in my hand.

We looked at it together. I was adorable in my polka-dot one-piece suit, pageboy haircut, eyes squinting into the sun.

"You look like I did," Mom said. "Except I have blue eyes."

Maybe there was hope after all. We'd looked like family, until, of course, I got fat.

I handed her a piece of candy as reinforcement. She bit into it with delight.

We used to spend every summer at the beach while my father stayed in the city, working. Most of the time I was alone digging up sea creatures and making drip castles with wet sand. I remember exactly when that picture was taken. How could I forget?

After capturing a big crab stuck in a tide pool I'd turned around and Mom was gone. I climbed the hill, pail in hand

and entered our silent rented beach house. I was always scared of losing her because already I understood that I was the last person she wanted to spend time with.

"Mom, Mommy," I shouted. "I found a big crab."

I heard laughter coming from her room. I tiptoed on the sandy wood floor to surprise her. She must have been talking on the phone.

Instead, she was lying in bed when I walked in, sharing a cigarette with a handsome lifeguard named Walt.

"You little shit," Walt shouted. "Don't you know how to knock?"

"I found a crab," I said, ignoring him. "Can I keep it?"

"We'll have him for dinner," Mom said, nudging Walt. They had both pulled the white sheets up to their chins, so it was like they were silly kids looking at me from inside a tent. Walt laughed. I decided to hate him even though he was the only person who ever talked to me when I played on the beach.

But at least I knew Mom was joking about dinner. Crab made her sick.

"I mean as a pet," I said.

"Get out of here, Elizabeth," she said. Walt stood up, naked, and pushed me out the door. I heard it lock.

Now I put the photo of me with the crab bucket on the table beside Mom's hospital bed.

"Remember the crab I found that day?" I asked her.

"No," she said, reaching her hand out for another chocolate.

I dug through the photos to show her the surefire breakthrough winner, a framed photo of her at about the age I'd been in the last shot, standing in front of the waves with her tall, handsome dad, her favorite person in the world.

I patted her on the hand. I knew that her father had been having "problems" at the time. In other words, he was going mad.

When I picked out the picture, I'd hoped my empathy would move her to take me to heart. I'd be somebody who knew her pain, somebody connected to her dad.

She pulled her hand away.

"Your hands are cold," she said.

Her eyes began to close. Her mouth opened a little and I could see that her tongue was covered with the dark candy. It looked like an evil cave.

"Don't you want to talk about your dad? How much you loved him?"

"That's enough for now," she said.

I felt a chill. Maybe she was sicker than I thought. Maybe I'd pushed her too hard. The therapist had been right: way down deep, I'd always believed everything was my fault, Mom's crappy personality and her lack of affection.

I didn't deserve her love.

And now I'd probably missed the healing moment for good.

I shouldn't have left before they brought her lunch. I'd promised Doreen I'd stay and cut her meat into teeny tiny pieces so she wouldn't choke.

"You can't trust the nurses to do that," Doreen had said. "They're too busy with the sicker people on the floor."

But I decided not to worry. Mom's teeth were still sharp.

"When will Doreen be back?" she murmured as I bent down to kiss her forehead goodbye.

She jumped slightly as my lips touched her skin. I never kissed her near her mouth. She didn't like that. Germs, she said.

"Later today," I said, stepping away from her. "She needs a rest."

"She's going to wheel me to the gift shop to see if there's anything new," Mom whispered. She loved to shop more than anything in the world.

And then she was asleep. She probably wouldn't remember I'd been there at all.

Feeling like a smelly, friendless bag lady, I walked down the hall with my photos. But then a couple of nurses and an orderly said hello to me and a patient even waved from her bed. There was a lovely spring flower arrangement at the nurses' station and over the loudspeaker somebody announced free smoothies in the cafe. On the cardiac floor, lunch was being served and the daily schedule was zipping along.

Things were getting better.

I even thought about going back to Mom's room. I didn't want her to choke and die because of me. But, instead, I kept walking as if leaving her alone was all the breakthrough I'd get.

Mom didn't die that day in the hospital. A week later, Doreen found her dead at home in front of the TV, still watching Katie Couric telling the news.

"Mommy is gone," Doreen said, wailing. I remember thinking, thank god somebody's crying.

"You handle the funeral arrangements, would you?" I said.

"Of course," Doreen said. And she did. She really did.

The "Celebration of Life" was held a week later at my mother's home, a beautiful place with its own private beach.

Toasting her with Möet, the mourners—the lawyer, the accountant, the jeweler, the cleaning woman, the nail girl, the car detailer—reminisced about Mom, her wry sense of humor and her zest for life. I spilled a little bubbly on the enlarged photo of Mom (slightly pregnant with me) that Doreen had made to stand next to the lovely Chinese urn filled with her ashes.

"Here's to you, Mom," I said, almost knocking over one of the huge sprays of lilies the accountant had sent.

"Toast," the sycophantic silver-haired husband of her college roommate called out. He'd been her lawyer forever and I assumed he'd been skimming her trust fund the entire time.

"Yes, yes," the nail girl, her mouth full of crab sushi, mumbled.

"She still had such a beautiful thick head of hair," Harold, the hairdresser, said. "What a loss."

"Such a sweet old gal," the car detailer, a ruddy ex-surfer named Ray, said. He opened another bottle of champagne and refilled everybody's glass.

I was getting too drunk and so was Doreen. We had to hang on to each other to stand up. I noticed the nail girl slipping a Swarovski parrot from the bookcase into her purse but I couldn't do anything about it. Everything seemed to be rolling like slow waves on a sunny day.

"Here's to you, Mommie Dearest," I toasted again.

"Dearest Mom," Doreen whispered wetly into my ear.

Taking full delight in the irony, Mom used to sign all her birthday cards to me "Love, Mommie Dearest." To her, Joan Crawford was a joke and a hero at the same time.

"Here's to Dearest Mom," I said, lifting my glass.

"I didn't know she had a daughter," said the jeweler. "She had a poodle named Princess once."

"Princess," the accountant said. "Princess died years ago."

"Time to send Helen to…" I paused.

"Heaven," Doreen said.

"Heaven," I said. "Hope there's a Nordstrom in heaven." I started laughing as if this was the greatest joke I'd ever heard.

"To Nordstrom," Doreen said, raising her glass.

"Who are we kidding?" I said then. "She's going straight to hell. She told me it sounded like it was much more fun."

With that there was silence. And then a couple of groans and then laughter and applause. The mourners knew my mother liked a nasty joke even if most had never heard of me.

And then I kissed her photo on the lips, a big wet smooch. It was the first time I'd ever been able to do that and it felt good even if she was only in black and white.

That was the last thing I remember from the Celebration of Life.

The next morning I woke up fully clothed on top of my mother's bed next to Doreen. In the middle of the night I'd thrown up in Mommy's toilet but other than that things could have been worse. My head didn't feel too bad and I had this jazzy sense of freedom even though I was still in my mother's house.

Sure, the memorial had been as absurd as any French farce, but in a way that was completely fitting. In life my mother had been ridiculous; in death she was no more than a cartoon. It was sad really.

But I wasn't. I padded out of the bedroom, leaving Doreen asleep, and went to survey the damage. Other than the mess of empty champagne bottles and flutes, everything looked OK. My mother had so many mermaid statues and mounted conch shells, glass figurines and South American butterflies captured in plexi-glass that losing a dozen tchotchkes to mourner theft didn't make a dent.

Objects were much more real to her than any human being, even Doreen.

But I wasn't about to let that thought get me down. Mom was gone and that was all there was to it. No more therapy. No more flag waving to get her to notice me. No more wishing she was dead.

I told myself I was ready to remake myself into somebody other than Helen's invisible daughter even if we'd missed the breakthrough when she was alive.

I walked out to the deck. Another beautiful day. Another beautiful view, even better than the one from the cardiac unit.

If Mom had left me the house, I'd start with the remodeling right here, adding a Jacuzzi and a fire-pit, maybe a sleek bar and some teak chairs. Then I'd knock down the wall between the dining room and the kitchen, sell the furniture and upgrade all the appliances.

I'd make this place mine.

Maybe I'd get into shopping just like Mom. I'd join a gym and lose weight. I'd get a better girlfriend, one who'd last.

Next door people were shouting at each other. "Where were you last night?" a woman yelled.

"Fuck yourself," a man said back.

Or maybe I'd sell it. I needed the dough, that was for sure. Mom never gave me a cent except for a couple of fifties in a gift card on holidays.

The neighbors were a wealthy young-ish couple with three sons, all named after Republican presidents, who were invariably kind to my mother, as if she was a normal old woman, a sweet gal who enjoyed children.

Mom knew how to play the part.

They hadn't come to her memorial, even though Doreen had invited them. Trouble in paradise. The idea made me smile, which was something my mom would have done, too.

I went inside and turned on the radio, loud, to the jazz station. Mom didn't have any CD's. Music wasn't really her style. She read the comics in the morning and watched the news and sitcoms at night.

Sonny Rollins filled the house with new energy. I twirled around a couple of times and then picked up a Lalique statue of a ballet dancer in blues and greens.

"Oh, look Mom," I said to the photo still standing next to her sealed urn. "Your favorite statue." I dropped the thing on the marble floor where it shattered. "Woops."

I took a pastel of her favorite poodle off the wall and smashed it over a chair.

"Woops," I said again. "Princess is all torn up."

I would have continued except that the Princess picture bumped Mom's cremation urn, which crashed to the floor and broke.

"Oh, good god," I screamed. "Mom."

I sat down next to the ceramic shards and looked for evidence of her. Where the ashes should have been was air, and dust. Nothing.

TWO

◆

Doreen was watching me from the doorway.

I walked to her and yelled in her face.

"What have you done with her? She isn't really dead, is she? You've taken her away. You murdered her and cut up her bones."

"She's frozen," Doreen said, yawning.

I ran into the kitchen and emptied the freezer. She followed me with one of my mother's bathrobes wrapped around her clothes.

I held up a baggie of white meat.

"What did you do with her?"

"That isn't your mother, Elizabeth. That's organic chicken breasts."

She started to grind some coffee.

I grabbed her arm.

"Don't mess with me, Doreen," I said.

"OK, OK. It's a surprise," she said, facing me. "I was going to tell you any minute now. You're right. Helen isn't completely dead. We made a plan last year to have her body frozen if she died. But it's a secret from everybody except you."

She handed me a business card from the pocket of Mom's robe.

"Stillwaters Cryonics Institute," it read. *"We put the life back into death."*

"You're kidding," I said. "She's dead-ish?"

"I thought you'd be so happy. Maybe you'll get to love her all over again. She left herself to you."

"Of course she did," I said. "I'm never getting away."

Doreen handed me a cup of coffee.

"You're the heir. Blood is thicker than water. I'd take responsibility for her body if I could. You know how close we were."

I didn't trust Mom in the least. And now I wasn't trusting Doreen much either. I tossed my coffee in the sink.

"Go visit her at Stillwaters," she said sweetly. "You'll feel better. They have her all dressed up."

What I learned on the creepy and surreal cryonics web site the next morning was that I didn't need to worry about Mom getting a second chance anytime soon. Technology was evidently nowhere near reviving frozen bodies. Rumors about Ted Williams' torso and Walt Disney's head notwithstanding, I was pretty sure Mom was doomed to be a big human block of ice for decades to come.

So, newly calm and confident, I visited Mom at the cryonics place. I told myself it might be interesting to have a look at her dead, in bed. That's the way I chose to think of the Plexiglas drawer David Emerson pulled out after I told him who I was.

He was the owner/host at Stillwaters. Over the phone he'd told me to come between the six and eight p.m. viewing hours.

Instead of being icky like the Internet site, Stillwaters revived me. The waiting room was filled with water sounds; there were several gurgling fountains and even a waterfall filling one entire wall. I wondered if the design had been David's idea, intended to subliminally remind us that ice melted, that death could become life.

"How do you like it, Ms. Pruitt?" he asked.

I'd imagined Stillwaters to be something halfway between cold storage and Dr. Frankenstein's lab. What I found was more like a minimalist Japanese airport hotel where the walls were covered with cubicles stacked one on top of the other but without the amenities: the clock, tiny TV or bathrooms down the hall.

"Is that the sound of waves?" I asked.

"Caribbean surf. Too artificial?"

"Not at all," I said. "What's reality got to do with a place like this?"

"We just love your mom," he said then, pulling out her drawer. The top was clear so we both could see her face, and although her eyes were closed "to prevent corneal damage," the rest of her looked as good as new. In fact, she didn't look a day over sixty-five or seventy. Her hair had been retouched to its original auburn, and on her face was the warmest smile I'd ever seen.

"Something tells me she likes it here," I said, getting into the swing of things. It seemed like everybody was floating in that pre-dawn moment before waking up from a deep sleep. I almost expected to see Mom's eyelids twitch from a vivid dream.

"She looks almost…"

"Alive?"

"Not exactly. More like warm. In life she was rather cold."

That, of course, was a colossal understatement. I don't think I'd ever seen my mother cry, even when her own mother, Hedda, ex-child star, died of old age. Even when my father left her for another woman, one who could love him back.

I swayed slightly and leaned on her drawer.

"Sorry," I said.

"Don't give it a second thought." He steadied me with a practiced and graceful hand. "Happens all the time on the first visit. You'll get used to the suspended look."

"You mean people visit here often?"

"It depends, Ms. Pruitt. For some it's more fulfilling to talk to a body than an urn or a mound of dirt or a photograph."

"Or that person alive," I said.

He raised an eyebrow.

"Kidding, kidding. Listen, call me Elizabeth, would you?"

"OK. I'm David."

I stood up to look at Mom more closely. She was dressed in her favorite lavender pantsuit with the biography, honest to god, of Joan Crawford tucked under one arm.

"Her caregiver said she'd wanted to get to Joan's book when death interrupted," David told me.

Now, as I glanced down at Mom, for a moment I thought I saw her wink. I tapped on the glass with my fingernails. Was she actually puckering her lips into a kiss? Was she trying to tempt me into bringing her back?

Suddenly I knew what I had to do. Before it was too late. Before somebody figured out the actual science for reanimation.

"David," I said firmly, "what can we do about shutting down the refrigeration and letting her go?"

"You mean die? We don't use that word here, Elizabeth."

I shivered with pleasure. It was finally payback time.

"Whatever," I said smoothly. "This is an unnatural and expensive self-indulgence. She was a rotten human being the first time around. Everyone knew it, although she paid them well to take care of her needs and pretend otherwise. Now if she were Princess Diana or Mother Teresa or something—"

"No can do," David interrupted. "We have a signed contract."

I decided to try the truth.

"Listen," I said, "my mom always made me feel like nothing. If I could just keep her dead, I might have a chance at life."

"Sorry," he repeated annoyingly. "No can do."

"What if I don't pay the rent?"

"Withholding funds is unethical, immoral and illegal, my dear."

"But there's no possibility of bringing her back for a long time, is there? That's what it said on the Internet."

David paused to fiddle with something on Mom's drawer.

"Well actually," he said finally, "for those select individuals..."

"You mean?" I gasped, unable to finish my sentence.

"Yes," David said. "The technology is in place, and people are already coming back. But we can't let the information out, or the government would shut us down and appropriate the whole thing. Politicians and priests are the only people who get to play God in this world."

"So it's all about who can afford the procedure," I said, everything inside me sinking.

"Let me show you something," David said, taking me by the shoulders and leading me over to one of Mom's roommates. He pulled out a drawer that held the body of a handsome man in his late twenties.

"Who's this?" I said.

"This is Raoul, my boyfriend. I'm going to bring him back, just like your Mom."

"My mother was not like a girlfriend," I said. "Haven't you been listening?"

"Between the lines, my dear," he said. This guy was too much.

Raoul's body was awful and wonderful at the same time. He was dressed in full drag as Little Bo Peep, bonnet and all.

"He died of an embolism at our last Halloween Party. Every year he dressed as a different female storybook character. Two years ago he was Red Riding Hood. Don't you love his curls?"

They were pretty. Long, golden tresses peaking out from under his hat.

"Why haven't you brought him back yet?" I asked.

"For personal reasons I want to age progress him," David said mysteriously. "We haven't perfected that part of reanimation yet. But your dear mother wants to age regress, to come back as a young girl. We're almost ready to try it. She'd be our inaugural procedure and you'd get to raise her."

I couldn't breathe. The air was stuck in my chest like a balloon.

"No," I croaked. And then I did the only thing I could. I took off and started running away from Mom's room, down white halls, past doors marked "Private," "Body Refrigeration," "Head Removal," "Melting Vat," horrible gothic things written in black and white as if they were as normal as "Oncology" and "Surgery". At the end of the last hall there was a bright light, like people describe in near death experiences. I pushed open the swinging door and found myself not in the hands of God, but in a kitchen full of chefs and their helpers chopping the heads off big fish.

"Elizabeth, stop," David called out in a big deep voice.

"I'll block her, boss," said a guy who looked exactly like Heath Ledger with a white chef's hat covering his messy hair.

I dodged him nimbly and pushed open another swinging door.

In front of me were diners, quietly ordering or eating, in an upscale restaurant painted in blues and greens.

Finally I stopped running. Where else was I going to go?

"This is Aquarium," David said behind me, "My restaurant. Let's go sit down at a table."

He took my elbow and led me to a quiet place in the corner.

The restaurant's interior didn't help how crazy I felt. One whole wall was filled with an aquarium. That was evidently the gimmick, pick your own fish and eat it. Crustaceans were aimlessly crawling around with their big claws and shells, crashing into each other. Ignoring them, big silvery fish teemed and floated, unaware of their impending doom.

I bent over to catch my breath.

"Would you like to see a menu?" said our waiter, a dead ringer for Rodney Dangerfield.

"Are you...?" I looked up at him.

"We'll start with the Beluga caviar," David said. "And champagne."

Rodney left, chuckling at something, maybe one of his old jokes.

"You're right. That was Rodney Dangerfield working as a waiter," David said. "And Heath Ledger in the kitchen. The reanimated work here as long as they want, until they get steady on their feet. There's a whole secret network of doctors and others supportive of our cause who help smooth the way back."

"This place, these people, the fish, this news. I thought reanimation was just a futuristic fantasy. All of a sudden it's a possibility. I'm sweating. It's possible I'm having a heart attack."

"Calm down, Elizabeth," David said. "Aquarium is supposed to be a haven for our customers and their families. Breathe in and out some more."

"Listen, buddy," I said. "You just told me we might be reanimating the almost worst person in the world. Give me a little break."

The caviar was delivered in a crystal bowl surrounded by perfect tips of toast. The champagne was Schramsberg. My mother would have loved this place.

"Now, now," he said to me, checking the menu. "It's going to be fine. Let's order. I'll have the pickled stingray." He winked at me. "It goes without saying that the poisons have been removed. And the octopus puree, although I do love sucking the cups. Maybe broiled instead."

"Raw starfish?" I said when it was my turn. "Battered blowfish? You're kidding."

"Try them both," David said. "Live a little. Walk on the wild side."

As I sipped the bubbly I tried to relax and allow myself to imagine what bringing Mom back might be like. No matter which way I looked at it, it was a nightmare.

Like in the movie *Saw*, I'd rather cut off my own leg. If she were the same it would be terrible. If she was different, possibly a kid, that would be just as bad but in a new way.

Reading my mind, he said, "This is about hope and change and second chances. Better get prepared. The doctors say the age regression procedure will be ready in a few months."

"My mother was never a sweet old lady who loved me. She'd never be a nice kid no matter how well I raised her. She'd never want me to have anything. Everything would always be just for her. I'd be worse off than the caregiver. I'd be ..." I paused. What would I be?

"You'd be her daughter," David said.

"I don't want her back," I said firmly. "At any age."

"I'm afraid you don't have a choice."

He smiled at me in a scary, knowing way.

"Everybody has a choice."

I was inordinately proud of my stand. I was strong. I was going to reinvent myself without Mom, the way relationships were supposed to work when somebody bad died.

When the food was served, Rodney stood by, waiting to see if it was OK. He was wearing a black suit and the signature Aquarium running-salmon tie. He looked good, not exactly age-regressed, but a bit less droopy around the eyes, as if freshened somewhat by the experience of resting on ice and then coming back to a calmer world in which he'd already finished with the business of fame.

"Got a joke, Rod?" David said.

"Sure boss," he said. "It's short and sweet."

We sat back to listen.

"What a childhood I had. Why, when I took my first step, (ta da) my old man tripped me."

We applauded and Rodney kissed my hand.

The battered blowfish wasn't half bad.

David told me after lunch that Mom had left a video will in her wall safe at home. He gave me the combination and made me promise to watch with an open mind. I figured I could at least do that. What did I have to lose by watching a movie made by my dead mom?

THREE

◆

The next morning I drove to her home, past the guard at the gate who waved me on, as if I owned the place, which, I figured, I would soon enough.

All my redecorating fantasies to the contrary, I didn't think I could bear to really live there myself, not with all the wealthy Republican neighbors, and every child on the beach blonde with their little silver beach shovel clutched in their hands. Plus, although I hadn't had a relationship since Minerva, I was officially a lesbian, and thus, in this beach community some kind of a monster, Ellen and Rosie notwithstanding.

I myself lived in the semi-gay, multi-ethnic hills where we had a good view of any marauders storming us from the flats. Plus, what wealthy straight Republican with children could be bothered pushing a stroller up and down narrow winding streets that run with rivers of rain water every time it storms? People actually spoke Spanish where I lived and made friendly gestures of multi-lingual greeting.

The neighbor wife who'd been fighting with her husband during Mom's memorial actually came out of her house when I parked to make sure I wasn't a thief.

"Hi," I said to the gal, a harried blonde, holding a cell phone to her ear.

No response.

"Hi," I said again. "I'm Helen's daughter, her heir."

"Dwight, just do what the teacher says even if it doesn't make sense," she said into the phone. "We'll talk about it when you get home."

"So, thanks for watching out for the house," I said.

"Your mother was a great gal," she said after snapping her cell shut. "I didn't know she had a child."

"I am..." I said, but she'd already turned toward her house without shaking hands or introducing herself. "...Elizabeth," I finished, towards her back. And then of course I felt like a fool.

Did I look too butch or too poor? My hair was short and my Honda was vintage, but this gal was too snooty even for here.

Thank god I hadn't reached out my hand.

Like I said, Mom wasn't generous with her dough—not with me, the starving poor or even the fancy university her parents paid her to go to. The only place to which she ever donated was the ASPCA and I think that was only because they sent her free return address stamps and that calendar she liked.

I think she also enjoyed having me beg every few years when I had a big medical bill or the plumbing in my house went out. She acted like she alone deserved the income from her trust fund just for being herself.

No more of that. Now I'd have enough to buy a new car and maybe even take a trip somewhere, to recover from my loss, as they say. And if I got sick, I could afford to go to the doctor, imagine that.

It was bizarre going into her house with nobody else around. The air was hot and dead. I was almost scared.

I tried to think about being rich myself.

Somebody would love this place when it sold. I'd have to get rid of all Mom's crap first, though. The stuffed animals and gilded statues couldn't ruin the view, but they did detract from the bones of the place.

It didn't work.

In the living room, the ghost of Mom grabbed me and shook me until I had to sit down on the couch, a floral job with the towel still on the place where Mom mostly sat, "in case of accident."

It all came over me– the resentments, the empty feelings, the relief and the loss. I stayed there for a while, crying a little bit and aching all over. It was so unfair that she had given me so much pain when she was alive and now that she was dead, I had to feel awful too.

But I was convinced that these feelings were better than the alternative David was trying to sell me–the magical reincarnation invented for the lucky few who could afford the trip.

When I could stand up, I went into the kitchen to get a drink. The ghost was there too.

"Hi Mom," I said to myself. I opened the beer and some of the mail that had been piling up. I used the same sharp letter-opener she'd always had on hand.

I finished with the mail and the beer and then I remembered her joke.

"Be careful you don't fall down on that and pierce your heart," I'd said as she limped over to the kitchen table with the knife and her bills. That's the way we talked. Our entire relationship was one mean laugh after another.

"Who says I have one?" she'd answered without missing a beat.

A few minutes later, after I set up the TV with the video and opened an expensive bottle of wine I'd found in the refrigerator, I lay down on Mom's bed. I looked in the bedside table and found all her pills right there within reach.

I pushed a couple of buttons and the film began. Imagine flowers and birds, funereal music in the background, chipper but eternal, and then, floating across the screen:

"The Living Will of Helen Pruitt, 1932 - ?"

The background faded away, replaced by Helen who was seated next to her freezer drawer, one arm lying on top of it possessively, the other holding a martini.

I took a long pull from the Pinot Grigio (who needed a glass?) and then fingered a bottle of Mom's pain pills. I was definitely feeling pain and something darker too. Was there a pill for that? In any case, I was glad for the Vicodin sitting next to me like the statue of a little Buddha.

Mom's first words to the camera were, "Doreen, light me." Mom put down her martini on a little table and reached out with a cigarette. An arm appeared from stage left with a lighter.

And then, "No, Mrs. Pruitt. There's no smoking." And David's arm from stage right removing it.

"Oh for God's sake," Mom said as the camera was readjusted.

"Do I start?" Mom said then. "OK, Elizabeth, if you're watching this now I guess I'm dead and frozen, a 'Momsicle'."

"Good one, Helen," Doreen laughed offstage.

"But seriously, I know you thought I was a bad mother."

"You got that right," I said, and popped my first pill.

Mom took a sip of her martini and draped her other arm back over the plexiglass bed.

"Your father wanted children, so I had you for him. And then it was hard to get good help so I might have been a little impatient. Sometimes you cried a lot—colic or whatever they called it."

Now she paused to empty her martini. She held up her glass, gesturing for more. Doreen reached across the camera with a shaker and filled the glass.

"Well anyway," Mom said, already slurring her words a little bit. "Get over it. We all had our problems growing up."

"Mine were worse," I said and swallowed another five pills with some more of the wine.

"My father committed suicide. Your father only ran away with his secretary. Good riddance to him. His bitch turned out to be a big drunk and fat. But you know all that."

David's hand appeared in the corner of the screen, making a motion for Mom to hurry up.

"OK, OK," she said. "Here's the plan. You'll receive the house and all my money if you bring me back and become my guardian. And if Stillwaters can make me young again I want to go to Bentwood Academy. I hear enrollment is tight so get on it right away."

I put my hand over my mouth. It was blackmail; I should have known she would have thought of that. She'd made David her trustee so she could manipulate me without anybody finding out.

And what choice did I have? If I wanted the money I had to take my mom with it. Otherwise, she'd probably figured out a way to leave it all to the ASPCA.

Shit.

David handed her a piece of paper, obviously some sort of prompt. The camera kept rolling while Mom put on her reading glasses.

Then, as if she could read my mind, Mom continued.

"Stillwaters insists on the cooperation of the next of kin when they do an age-regression, so you're all I've got. A little touch of financial pressure just assures me that we have a future together. You probably haven't planned for your retirement or inevitable medical bills, have you?"

She paused for a small smirk at the camera and a final sip of her martini. Then smiling hugely, she went in for the kill.

"I promise I'll grow up to be the best mother you ever had. God is giving us another chance, Elizabeth. You can't say no to God. Close up, please."

The camera obligingly moved in on her face.

Honest to god, there was a tiny tear in the corner of her right eye.

"I love you, Elizabeth. Let me come back to show you how much."

While the credits and butterflies were still running I took all the rest of the pills. I lay down flat, closed my eyes, and pretty soon I felt something very heavy on my chest, like a cat or a small dog. At first the weight almost kept me from catching my breath but soon whatever it was became comforting and warm. And then I fell asleep.

FOUR

◆

When I woke up my head was drumming and my mouth tasted like sour milk. I was also hearing voices, the strangely disembodied sound of words spoken over a public address system.

I opened my eyes. I was in a room filled with intense daylight, the wallpaper covered with those pastel brushstrokes of paint.

I was in a hospital. The room was just like the one my mom always had.

And then I remembered. All those pills. How could I still be alive?

I turned my head. The answer was sitting in a chair to my left, her chin on her chest, snoozing. She must have stopped by and found me passed out on Mom's bed.

Doreen couldn't let my mother stay dead and she wouldn't let me die.

"I guess I should thank you," I said.

I noticed she'd put a framed photo I'd never seen next to my bed. It was my Mom as a child in a darling pastel portrait, her soft brown hair in a pageboy, her smile open and sweet. And, of course, those eyes, blue and clear.

Doreen woke up and looked at me for a moment like she couldn't remember who I was.

"Oh," she said, wiping her eyes. "You were so sad about your mother's dying that you took all her pills."

"Doreen, stop kidding yourself. We can't bring her back. After watching her talk to me on that damn video will, I realized I'd rather be dead and poor than saddled with her. That's how bad it would be. "

Doreen patted my hand as if she was my friend. I knew better. She was so in love with my mother's return and I was the wet nurse.

"Listen, Elizabeth, it will be wonderful."

I jerked my hand away and picked up the photo.

"Who painted this portrait? I've never seen it before."

"A friend of mine," she said. "I gave her a childhood photo and she added a few of her own touches. The original is hanging over my fireplace. I hope you don't mind. I thought it might make you feel better to see Mom this way."

"She didn't like me in the least," I said. "This adorable child can't change that."

"She couldn't help it," Doreen said. "She had bad help; you cried a lot. It will be different this time, I promise."

"That's not true. I only cried when absolutely necessary."

At this moment, a nurse named Pammi came in to take my vitals and Doreen slipped out, blowing me a kiss. She left the photo behind.

"I know you," Pammi said. "You have that mother. She was always in this room too."

"She died," I said.

Pammi slapped a cuff over my arm.

"I'm so sorry," she said, looking at me closely to check if I was still suicidal.

"Don't be," I said. "What a bitch she was. Probably to you too."

Pammi finished with my blood pressure and then suggested we go for a little walk while we waited for the psychiatrist to sign me out.

"You need some happy pills?" she asked as we strolled down the hall, me pushing the IV between us. "Now is the time to tell Doctor. The psychiatrists like to prescribe meds even to the overdosers."

I laughed. Was this informal interview part of the sign out procedure?

"You're cute, Pammi," I said. She was. She had blue eyes and a thick blond braid like a Scandinavian tennis champion. "But aren't you busy? Shouldn't you be doing something else? You don't have to entertain me."

"You're my excuse to look at the babies."

"I don't really care about newborns," I said.

"You should," she said, waving her pinky at a little kid named Aaron, in the first row.

Then her beeper went off.

"Gotta run, darn it," she said. "Can you find your way back?"

"Why should I care about newborns?" I called after her but she was gone.

I turned my attention back to the babies. I know it was probably from the medication still in my blood stream but I could swear they were all wearing Mom's face, even Aaron.

"One of these yours?" a woman wearing a tweedy wool suit said. She'd slipped up next to me while I was channeling Mom.

"No," I said. "I don't have any children."

"I have three myself," she said. "That's my little niece over there." She pointed and I pretended to know which one to admire.

"Cute," I said. "Cute, cute, cute."

"I think being a parent is the most important thing you can do," she sighed. "You're shaping the life of an entire human being. It's all about hope."

One of the babies yawned. Another, with the pinched up face of an old man, jammed his fist in his mouth and began to cry. He looked so adorable that for a moment I almost wanted to grab him up and run for it.

Minerva had always wanted a baby. Maybe she'd had a point.

They all stopped looking like Mom.

Or maybe the doctor had already put me on happy pills and I was just zonked with bliss.

The idea of raising a child began to seem marvelous, even if it was Mom as the kid. How hard could it be to teach her to love me?

"Oh, to hell with it," I said. "How bad a parent could I be?"

"Excuse me?" said the gal in wool.

Besides, as the biological adult in the relationship, I'd have all the power and the money.

"I am going to have a baby. I just found out."

She glanced at my IV.

"No complications, I trust."

"Aren't there always?" I said and marched to my room to sign up for whatever new pills would make me brave enough to bring Mom back as a kid.

The shrink didn't show up for awhile, so I sat down on the visitor's chair by the bay view window, but I couldn't see a thing. No sailboats or setting sun behind Catalina Island, no seagulls or kayakers. Only gray clouds and sad silver water. I began to sniffle. I can hardly stand to admit it but now that I'd made up my mind, I actually missed my mother.

When the shrink, Doctor Snyder, finally arrived, he briskly told me that I hadn't taken nearly enough pills to kill myself, like he was disappointed.

"It was an impulse overdose in honor of my mother," I said. I knew he wasn't listening. He'd unhitched me from the IV and was already doing his paperwork.

"Well, whatever," he said handing me a few forms. "Medication and the number of a grief group. You need somebody to talk to? You have an interest in life?"

"Like a hobby?"

Snyder had wire-rimmed glasses, a thin patrician nose and white hair. I thought about how much he must hate having to do rounds in a hospital with people like me– malingerers and time wasters.

"Like anything."

"I might have a child."

"Really?" He looked at me over the top of his glasses, like what a bad idea a baby was for somebody as screwed up as me.

"Adoption," I said. "I know what you're thinking, but this one little slip shouldn't disqualify me. There are so many unwanted children out there. There must be plenty of worse parents than me."

Doreen arrived then from the cafeteria with a cup of coffee for me. Then she pushed me out of the hospital in a wheel chair to drive me home. She let me carry the portrait of Mom on my lap.

"I can do the rest by myself," I said, when we got to my house.

"You sure?" she said.

"Sure," I said, getting out of the car. I tried to look efficient and independent, a person who was prepared to be alone but also supervise a reanimated child.

"I decided I'm going to bring Mom back," I said into her car window. "But I'm not doing it for you or her or David."

Doreen clapped her hands like a kid.

"I knew you would," she said. "You just had to get over the big bump."

"What big bump?"

"The big bump of your mind."

That was when I realized that if I was going to raise Mom up to be the right mother for me, the first thing I had to do was get rid of Doreen. She was a nice person with a lot of energy, but if she were around all Mom would ever be is a spoiled brat, the same as the old lady who just died.

FIVE

◆

They say the best part of everything is the anticipation. By the time David called three months later to tell me that Mom was due back the next week, age regressed, I'd signed her up for Bentwood School as my first cousin once removed, orphaned and Icelandic. I'd also fixed up the guestroom in my house for her with charming floral wallpaper, bought her a few returnable classic outfits in several sizes, studied my parenting handbook, and dreamed every night of future happiness.

I was hoping she'd come back as a baby, a blank slate, but David was being deliberately vague about her exact age.

"Younger," was all he would say.

I had her covered from infant to tween. I'd have to trust the process from there.

But the evening before her return, I was so nervous all I did was pace. I'd been in deliberate denial about the huge possibility of complications since I made my decision to bring her back. Now I finally had to let myself think about what Mom might be like when the life force started up in her again, no matter what age she returned. And what I would be like, too.

I intended to be a good guardian, of course, but I worried that those big needs I had might get the better of me. What if she still didn't like me or wasn't affectionate? Alternately, what if she lost her best qualities along with her worst? What if she wasn't smart or funny? What if she was a freak?

All the inheritance money in the world wouldn't be worth that heartache.

The next morning, I walked into the Stillwaters waiting room with a baby carrier, just in case she came back as an infant.

"She'll be older than that," David said gently.

"You didn't tell me exactly. You let me hope she'd be a blank slate."

"It's going to be wonderful no matter what age she is," he said. "It's the miracle of second chances."

Even though he had helped my mother try to blackmail me, I couldn't help but like this guy. I think he truly believed in his work. It was almost a spiritual calling. But I still had to wonder why he'd waited so long to bring back his boyfriend, Raoul. I figured we'd get to that later.

Now, I kicked the carrier into the corner and started to walk around the wood-paneled room, picking things up and putting them down.

A tiny carved horse in bronze, an abalone shell, a book about fly-fishing and finally, the requisite cryonics water sculpture, a simple glass bowl with a yellow and purple pansy floating in the middle.

"This reminds me of holiday dinners at Grandma Hedda's house," I said, dipping a couple of fingertips into the water. "At every setting the servants would place a crystal flower bowl for us to wash our fingers in between courses. Grandma was so rich she had two people to serve at each meal, plus the cook. My mother never worked a day in her life, not even in school. Her parents hired tutors who did the homework for her."

David patted the couch beside him.

"Calm down," he said. "Come sit beside me and breathe."

"She'll learn to work this time. Hard work is the key to everything. And the responsibility for taking care of animals." I sat down next to him but I couldn't stop talking. "I bought a parenting handbook. Schoolwork, household chores, riding lessons certainly, but she'll also groom the horse and clean its stall. How much longer do we have to wait?"

"I'll go check."

He left me alone then. I tried to sit quietly while I waited for my entire life to change. I imagined a future full of tenderness and mutual respect. Vacations together, heart to heart talks, shared dreams and, of course, shopping trips. I deserved at least that from my mom and probably a lot more.

I tried my damnedest not to allow bad memories or worries to pollute my thoughts, which I was beginning to think of as Mom's amniotic bath in my brain.

Finally, David and his two doctors came to the door and called me in to see my mom.

"It's wonderful," one of the doctors said. "She's beautiful and healthy, and those blue eyes with the spattering of freckles over the bridge of her nose are to die for. You'll be very proud. She's definitely our best reanimation so far."

The other doctor was beaming as well.

"The age regression worked beyond our wildest hopes! Like it was just meant to be. That sweet little soul in there just waiting for us to bring her back."

I laughed. Mom had put one over on them already.

But when we walked to the "Greeting Room" and I saw her, Helen, standing next to a nurse, I couldn't speak.

She was beautiful. A radiant vision of dewy youth.

"Elizabeth," David said sharply. "Say something to her."

"She's not a blank slate," I murmured. She was about ten or eleven years old and looked, in a pretty yellow party dress, just like the perfect girl in those photo albums from the old days.

This is the beginning of the rest of my life, I was thinking. I have to remember this moment forever.

The girl was staring vacantly at a point somewhere above my right ear.

I whispered, "What have we done?"

My spine tingled with the audacity of it. What good could come of defying nature this way?

But then the child looked at me with my mother's big blue eyes and I forgot all my second thoughts. This was no monster. This was the cutest, sportiest, smartest girl I'd ever seen.

When she ran toward me, wrapped her arms around my waist and rested her head against my stomach, I fell in love.

"Elizabeth, I knew you'd come," she said in my mother's same voice, but higher and smoother.

"Mom, of course I came. I've never been so excited. Now let me look at your toes."

"You silly," she said, but then she sat down and dutifully took off her Mary Janes and lacy socks to show me two perfect sets of five toes on each foot. I bent over and took one foot in my hand and smelled it like a precious truffle.

"You'd better sit down too, Elizabeth," my girl said, patting the chair next to her. I suddenly realized how different things were going to be. My old mom, as I was starting to think of her, would never have noticed whether I needed a chair; she'd never much noticed anybody outside of herself, and now here was this angel child, taking care of me.

"All right," I said, "Mom."

"Call me Helen, dear," she said. "Exactly how old am I? I can't quite tell. I must be only four feet tall, and I certainly don't have any breasts." She patted her chest experimentally.

"You're somewhere between nine and eleven," David answered her. "The doctors told me we couldn't be that specific going backwards."

"I feel so light and cheerful," Mom said, getting up and dancing a little tap with her brand new patent leather shoes. "My feet don't hurt and my knees don't ache. My whole life is ahead of me."

"You're the first to be brought back young," I said.

"I feel…" She paused. And then, sweet girl, she wept. "Thank you, Elizabeth. Thank you doctors and nurses and David."

The tears were real. I patted her lightly on the back and she reached out to hold my hand. I could hardly breathe for all the joy inside my chest.

"Now let's blow this Popsicle stand," Mom said, grabbing my hand. I laughed. Some of her old witty personality had evidently come back with her, untouched by time.

SIX

◆

The first thing she and I did together after leaving Stillwaters was to go get her burgundy Jaguar washed at my favorite place, a labor-intensive spot where they worked hard to please. Kids always like to go to the carwash, don't they? And, although I didn't exactly know how much of this little girl was still my mom, I was pretty sure the car had to be perfect for her to enjoy the rest of the ride.

At Suds and Seabreezes they let you stay inside during the first wash cycle, so I had to raise my voice over the sound of brushes and spray. Sheets of water slid over the windows almost as if we were actually under the ocean, moving along the sandy floor.

"What would you do if I opened the window right now?" Mom asked me, in a deeper voice than before, those blue blue eyes squinting like a devil, her hand on the door. I was shocked.

"Helen," I said. "Be good."

It was hard to call her Helen but it got easier when she was being bad.

"I'm sorry dear," she said, speaking higher all of a sudden. "I don't know what came over me."

"It's your car too. It's our only car you'd be ruining."

For a moment I wondered if Mom had been reanimated as a multiple personality, with old and young jockeying for control.

She backed off a little, thank god. With its fancy mahogany and leather interior, this car had made my first disciplinary challenge a snap. Even a spoiled kid knew better than to pour water all over the place. I'm pretty sure the editors of *Whole Parent, Whole Child*, the best-selling parenting handbook I'd studied, would have approved of my calm yet firm reminder.

Little Mom pouted for a moment, feet kicking the dashboard, arms across her chest. There was definitely a lot of my old mean mother left inside this cute girl. A tiny frisson of desperation rose up in my chest.

"Mom, are you going to be mostly well-behaved? Are you going to love me?" I said.

"What funny questions, Elizabeth." She said and sat up straight. "You startled me. What do you think? You're all I've got."

"I mean, isn't love why you wanted to come back?" I said. "Aren't we supposed to have this chance to fix our relationship?"

"Honey, I'm a little girl," she said. "I don't know all the answers yet. It's all mixed up in here." She pointed to her brain and smiled. I let it go. What else could I do?

We left the car with one of the finishing guys and sat on a bench to watch. It was our first public appearance together, and we seemed to be passing for normal just fine.

"What do those stickers on the bumper mean?" she asked me.

I'd put a couple of mine on as soon as I started to drive the Jaguar.

"Oh, you mean 'It's Never Too Late To Have a Happy Childhood'?"

"And 'Friends Don't Let Friends Vote Republican'?" she said.

"Jokes," I said. "You like jokes."

"Oh my god," she said. "Of course. You're a Democrat. You're gay too, aren't you? You've never had a boyfriend."

"We'll talk about it later," I said. Mom still didn't have one basic idea of who I was. Why was I surprised?

We sat in silence for a moment.

"I've never been to a carwash before," she said finally. "We had someone come once a week to do it at the house."

"I know," I said. "I met the detailer at your memorial."

"Could I have some of those?" She pointed towards the candy and Coke machine. "I'm famished. Where's all my money?"

"You don't have any," I said. "You gave it all to me. You're a child now."

"Do I get an allowance?"

"Later, in return for certain chores around the house."

She let it go. Another lucky break.

"I'd like to work here when I'm old enough. I could climb into the tight spots where the big guys don't fit, under backseats and, stuff. I bet they get to keep all the loose change they find."

"You'll earn ten dollars a week for emptying all the wastebaskets in the house."

"Why can't Doreen do it?" she asked.

"Because Doreen won't be around anymore, Helen. It's just you and me."

"Oh," she said.

Phew. So much for Doreen, her devoted companion of a dozen years.

"That's all I have to do?"

"You have to make your bed and water all the indoor plants too." If this girl wanted even more responsibilities, I'd give them to her, right away. The guy finishing our car waved his towel in the air, so we walked over to him to pick up our keys.

"You hand him his tip," I said and gave her a ten-dollar bill. She'd always been a notoriously bad tipper in her former life.

I patted her on the shoulder. She held out her hand so gracefully to this man with *Alvin* printed on his uniform you'd think she'd been meeting African-Americans for years. In reality the only black people she'd ever seen in her restricted beach community picked up the garbage.

"Pleased to meet you," she said. "I'm thinking of working here, too."

Alvin laughed and punched her lightly on the arm.

"Good sense of humor," he said.

It was all so strange it made me dizzy. Here I was standing next to my mother, a ten-year-old girl, who was handing the car wash guy a darn good tip, a better tip than she'd ever given anyone in her former tightwad life. I had to laugh.

"What's wrong?" she asked me as we drove away. "What's so funny?"

"Nothing," I said. After Alvin thanked us for the tip I asked him to come for dinner sometime. Now that I was sure she wasn't going to be my little angel, I wanted to introduce Helen to all walks of life, and this man seemed as good a place to start as any. Like my parenting book said, you have to actually teach kids empathy. Otherwise they might turn out to be psychopaths or pornographers or somebody like my original Mom.

To this end I was already making a list in my mind: Alvin first, and then a dying person, somebody disabled, retarded, crazy: an athlete, an artist, a liberal politician. For someone like Mom the possibilities for expanded empathy were endless. Before reanimation all she'd known were Republicans and household help.

"I'll give you five dollars to hit that fat cow," she said as we turned the corner on the way to my house. A lady in hair curlers was pushing a shopping cart across the street, huffing and puffing like a trooper.

It was something Mom used to say the first time around, about everybody who wasn't perfect in public.

She giggled hysterically, like a child possessed.

"Helen, damn it. That's Mrs. Samson, our neighbor."

"Which side does she live on?"

"What does it matter which side?"

"Not near my bedroom, I hope," she said. "I don't want to be seeing her every day when I get up in the morning. It might make me sick."

"Don't be such a bitch," I said. "Please."

"I think you've gained weight too, Elizabeth."

That was it. I snapped and made a U-turn in the middle of the road. The tires squealed.

"I'm taking you back to Stillwaters," I said. "A bad attitude when you're old and achy is one thing, but when you're an adorable kid it's punishable by death."

"Are you threatening me? Just because I said you'd gained weight?"

"You're a do-over. You're defective, a lemon. We'll refreeze you and bring you back the way I wanted, a blank slate, a baby."

"Elizabeth, I'm sorry to have to tell you this but in cryonic technology, you only get one chance to come back. Didn't David explain that the wiring burns out?"

"No," I said. "That doesn't sound scientific. You're making it up."

"You're not fat, darling," she said. "You are perfect. I don't know what came over me. I'm just so mixed up. You promise not to threaten me again and I promise to try harder."

"Try harder?"

"Not to say whatever comes into my mind."

She didn't talk much after that, even though there were plenty of fat and ugly pedestrians wandering around on the way back to our house. One big gal was jogging without a bra and a small man was walking a Great Dane. I waited but Helen didn't speak.

When we pulled in the driveway, I held my breath, waiting for some mean remark. But still there was well-behaved silence.

I'd bought the stucco cottage years before, at the height of the market, with Minerva/Min, aka goddess of wisdom and martial arts, an oxymoron if I ever heard one. I'd met her at a Diamond Dolls roller derby when she spilled her beer all over me. She was with a boyfriend but she managed to flirt with me like mad. She wiped the beer off my lap using just her hand and a small napkin.

"Here we are," I said.

"Really?"

"For awhile."

"We have the money for better, don't we?"

"Sure," I said, "but I thought we'd keep a low profile for a year or so."

"Low profile!" Helen said. "You're a lesbian." She might as well have called me a freak.

"Does it bother you so much if I am?"

"I'm flattered," she said surprisingly. "It means you turned to women because you really admired me, a woman myself."

I had to laugh. Typical Mom, turning things around to reflect well on herself.

"You laughed," she said. "Good. You've always been so sour."

Min left me and the house for another man about two years ago, which is when I started therapy. I hadn't had a date since.

"Yep," I said. "I'm a single lesbian and now I live with you."

The truth is that it was kind of a relief when Min left. The relationship had never gone much deeper than good sex and bad love. I mean she was beautiful, kind and all that. She was always telling me I was great. But that kind of stuff can get on your nerves. You start to wonder how good the other person is, if she thinks so much of you.

At least that's what I thought about it. The therapist had tried to encourage some couple's work but I wasn't interested. I mean my point of view is that once it's over, it's over.

Except with Mom, I guess.

"Do you have a job?"

"Yes," I said. "I own a house cleaning business called 'Elizabeth's Elves'."

The name was bad but it worked. People liked the idea of elves cleaning their house instead of poor women desperate to survive. At least my gals were documented and insured.

"Oh, that's nice."

So Mom understood nothing about my work or my life. And now that she knew I was a lesbian one of the worst things about her worked out in my favor. Nothing had changed. She still didn't give a shit. Nobody else in the world really mattered except her.

"It's not fancy but it's a friendly neighborhood and safe too," I said, waving at a middle-aged couple across the street from my house. "Those folks always move my garbage cans back for me after the truck goes by if I'm not home to do it myself."

It was a hilly middle class suburb full of gay and straight couples, hosing down their cars and walking their dogs. In the six years I'd owned the house, a short-sale bargain I'd gotten on a fluke, Mom had never been to visit me once.

"Who are those people you waved at?"

"The Garcias," I said. "He's a ..." and then I stopped. It made me mad to think I needed to justify my neighbors' worth by telling Helen about their good jobs.

"A what?" she said.

"A chemistry professor. She does something with computers." Of course, it shouldn't have mattered even if they were a gardener and a maid, but I figure Helen needed all the education I could give her.

We got out of the car. I braced myself. Who did I think I was bringing her back to this dump to live?

"Welcome home, Helen," I said. "I would have done balloons and a banner but we have to keep your re-emergence sort of low key, at least until we get used to creating our new life."

"It's not bad, not so bad," she repeated. "We'll get a landscaper and somebody to paint the walls. Maybe dark blue like in Acapulco. And plant some bougainvillea, pink and red. As if everything's been designed instead of thrown together this way and that."

"I can't believe you've never seen it," I said. "You really know nothing about me, do you? You've never been interested in a thing."

My voice was calm but my mother wasn't stupid. She could tell I was visiting my old childhood complaints.

"Oh, Elizabeth. Let's not go back over unpleasantries." She put her cold little hand in mine. "We had nothing in common."

"Never mind," I said. "Let's go in."

I turned on the light and gave her time to look around. It was better inside. I'd chosen good art for the walls and decent furniture for the rooms.

"Well, this is better than outside," she said, glancing around. "How much did you get for the beach house anyway?"

She missed her old place of course. I felt sorry for her in a way. Much worse to be wealthy and come down in the world than like me, suddenly loaded but without much interest in things material, just wanting financial security, I guess.

Besides, I was going to teach her how false and empty materialism and comforts were. We'd live in my somewhat shabby, threadbare house and enjoy each other, the beauty of nature and organic food.

I started to have some renewed hope and energy. Helen would be a challenge for the first few weeks while I reworked the crappy character stuff that seemed to be determined to reemerge.

"We'll stay here for awhile and try to blend in," I said. "Remember our cover story, the one we discussed at the carwash?"

"I'm your cousin's daughter going to Bentwood. My parents died in Iceland."

"I thought you might come back as a baby but I enrolled you as a sixth grader just in case. So that all works out."

"I like that painting," she said, ignoring me and pointing at the wall to my right.

"Of course you do," I said. "It's from your house."

It was a rocky scene of that same beach where I'd lost Mom when I was a little kid.

"Oh yes," she said. "For a moment it skipped my mind." She tapped herself on the head. "I think it's all in here though, all my memories. Your father, my mother, my father, and all the dogs I ever had."

"And me," I said.

"And you," she said.

Then she picked up a small black bowl I'd bought in Santa Fe.

"Indian," I said. "Sort of valuable. Gift from Minerva, an old girlfriend."

Minerva loved her ethnic arts and crafts. She'd told me her mother's family background was Blackfeet and her father's ancestors were conquistadors, as if your heritage made you more real and closer to the earth or something.

"What if I dropped it?" she said. "Would you be covered?"

"I'll show you your bedroom now," I said, ignoring the provocation.

She handed me the bowl and looked around her room. She loved it, thank god. She liked the bed's medium firm mattress, the lacy curtains, the teak desk and the rosy wallpaper. I let her jump on the bed for as long as she wanted.

"We'll go on a shopping spree and get me clothes and school supplies tomorrow," she said, lying down.

Before I could respond Helen's eyes were closed.

"What's for dinner?" she said.

"Steak," I said. "Baked potato, green beans. Ice cream and chocolate *Welcome Home* cake for dessert."

How could I go wrong with that?

"Sounds good," she said. "Wake me up when it's ready. I could eat the whole cow."

I felt inordinately gratified by that. The idea of actually feeding my mother so moved me that I almost overcooked the beef, fantasizing about all the good days ahead.

Later, after dinner, I put her to bed like you would any kid of eleven. I was thinking maybe we'd get to touch more now that she was a kid. I figured a little affection would be a slam-dunk given the fact that when she was old she'd always made Doreen turn off her light and kiss her on the forehead.

"Sweet dreams, Mom," I said, patting her on the arm.

Would she pull her arm away? Would she reach up for a quick hug?

"I wish I hadn't eaten so much," she said, belching lightly. "I have to remember that I'm smaller now. I don't want to get fat like..." Mercifully she stopped there.

I went to the end of her bed and waited.

She glanced my way.

"Oh, Elizabeth," she said. "Come over and let me kiss you. Thank you for everything you've done. We're going to have a wonderful life together. You'll see."

We kissed each other's cheeks drily and then she turned off the light and I was dismissed.

SEVEN

◆

We only had about a week to get Helen ready for school, to pass as a sixth grader with cool clothes and normal tween girly habits like texting and fainting over Justin Bieber. I had no idea how to coach her in any of it so I did the only thing I could think of. I called Minerva who was, after all, the closest thing to a straight friend I had.

And, best of all, she had an eleven-year old stepdaughter at Bentwood who had come as part of her marriage to Frank. The only problem was that Kendra was almost too hip. In fact she was African American, which I figured might be a problem for my old mom. But there was also a chance that maybe new Helen had forgotten to be racist. No matter what, the whole thing was bound to be another learning experience.

Ah Minerva. Would she be glad to hear from me? I'd tell her Helen was my poor dead cousin's daughter, I guess, the same as I was going to tell everybody else. Parents dead in Iceland due to volcanic activity and leave it at that. I could flatter her and

Kendra into coming with us on a shopping trip, though. All I'd have to do was mention Minerva's sense of style.

I'd also tell her I'd pay for lunch, just to clinch the deal.

So the four of us walked into Nordstrom the next day, two moms with their girls. "But she's black," Helen had said when I told her about Kendra. "She's going to pick out black people clothes. Is this a joke?"

"Oh, Helen," I said. "Be good. This is the only preteen I know. She's going to Bentwood. It's all about class, not race nowadays. She and her stepmother, Min, have money."

"So Min was your girlfriend and after knowing you she turned heterosexual?" Helen grinned evilly.

"Take off that face. You look like a bad carved pumpkin," I said. "I shouldn't have told you."

In a moment of giddy intimacy after dinner the night before, I'd been so flattered when Helen ate the grilled chicken I'd fixed that I began to tell her my recent life story including Minerva. Today, it was evidently still so funny, she had to mention it again.

In spite of all that, she and Kendra picked out cute dresses, shorts and shirts, even accessories, all appropriate for an approximately 11-year-old girl. And she made a friend out of Kendra, I don't know why. Maybe she guessed in advance she'd need some help with her math homework. She'd never in her life taken to anybody without a payoff.

"I think they might get along," I said to Minerva, as we walked to our cars carrying all Helen's packages like we were the help. Helen and Kendra were strolling in front of us drinking Cokes and discussing boys.

"Does that mean we have to see each other again?" Min said. I couldn't tell if she was joking. How pathetic that I'd stayed with somebody for three years when I couldn't even tell that much.

"No," I said. Min was trouble. She even smelled straight now, all dolled up with painted fingernails and perfume.

It was the perfume that always got me. This time it smelled musky, like cloves.

"Just kidding," she said, smiling with all that heterosexual privilege sitting on her shoulders like a magic cape.

"Hey, hurry up," Helen called. The girls were standing by the cars, hot and tired from all the fun.

"Ha, ha," I said.

"I still love you," she whispered while leaning in to kiss me on the cheek.

I pushed her away lightly. What an asshole she was, playing with me like I was a needy idiot. Min was making my old mother look good.

"That was very successful," Helen said to me on the way home, her purchases filling up the back seat of the car so I could barely see the traffic behind me. The trunk was so full we had to have her sit and bounce on it so that the latch would catch.

"Good," I said.

"Minerva seems really happy to spend time with her black stepdaughter. It's like they were made for each other."

I turned my head and looked at her. She was oblivious to how I might take her remark. When I was a kid she couldn't seem to get away from me fast enough.

"We're happy now too, aren't we?"

Why the hell did I keep asking her these questions?

"I think we're still growing into each other. It's only been a few days after all."

Tears filled my eyes. I could hardly see to drive.

"If Kendra's at Bentwood," she continued, "they must have integrated a lot since I knew it. She said she'd look out for me but I don't know."

"What do you mean?" I said, wiping my eyes with a Kleenex.

"You got something in your eyes?"

"No, Helen." We were driving past my favorite gelato place but damned if I'd stop there for her unless she got sweeter right away, unless she acted more as if she was glad to spend her new life with me.

"I mean, I don't think I want to go to school."

"What are you going to do all day while you're growing up again? You don't want to spend all your time with me. You have to try to pass as a kid."

Then it occurred to me that I still didn't really know why she'd come back. Logically, nobody wants to be dead unless they're suicidal or ill but there had to be something else too. I knew she hadn't come back to be with me or go to school.

Maybe now was the time for that conversation. I made a U-turn into Bianchi's Gelato. I figured our first big discussion would go better with dessert.

"I can eat all the sugar I want," she said to the teenaged server. He smiled at her because, even though she was eleven, she was cute. We sat at a table outside, in the sun.

"To be honest, I hoped to come back at seventeen," she said. "That was when I first fell in love, with a guy kind of like this gelato kid. Curly black hair, nice physique. Paul played lacrosse at the club."

"Wasn't that the year your father...?"

"Killed himself," she said resolutely. "It was a big scandal. It scared Paul Robbins away. Like a bird. I wanted to come back to fall in love again but this time with somebody who wouldn't run away."

She wiped a drop of the chocolate/blood orange gelato off her upper lip.

So there it was. The truth. Or part of it. And, of course, it had nothing to do with me. But still, I had to feel compassion for this girl attempting to do a major life-over. How many people have the means and imagination to try that? I'll bet not one other person in the world.

I ate my pistachio gelato in silence. We were both trying to rewrite history. And why not? We all want love, right? My mom wanted a better boyfriend and I wanted a mom.

"Well, Helen," I said finally. "We've got to be the best ten through sixteen we can and by seventeen maybe things will turn out better than last time."

"Oh, all right," she said. "But you have to do 'our' homework for me."

Some things never change.

EIGHT

◆

Two weeks after Helen started school, I got hauled into the principal's office. He was a tall, slender, elegant man about my age, the type of gentleman fancy prep schools seem to like, bow-tied Ivy League intellectuals.

"Hmm," Mr. Gibson said, shuffling through a sheaf of papers.

"What?" I said.

"Well, let's put it this way," he said finally, pushing his reading glasses to the top of his head. "Helen's doing some pre-adolescent testing of limits."

"And that means?"

"Well, her geography teacher caught her taking a cashmere sweater from the collection box. The class project is sending clothes and toys to a family in Botswana."

"What did she say?"

"Helen told her teacher that Africans don't need sweaters. That the climate is obviously too hot in that area for outerwear."

"Not a bad point," I said. "But rather cheeky."

Mr. Gibson just looked at me.

"It was stealing," he said, but his eyes were wet with mirth. "Listen, she's only in sixth grade."

I smiled happily. Helen's pre-teen academic career was inevitably going to be plenty shaky given her bad attitude and mental age. If Gibson liked us, found us funny, it might make all the difference.

"Yes," I said. "Absolutely. Anything else?"

"An issue with the art teacher about whose responsibility the paper and paint cleanup was. Helen seemed to think that's what the custodians are employed for. The discussion got pretty heated, I guess. The art teacher sent her to my office."

Now that wasn't funny. Helen's sense of entitlement was taking her way too far.

I looked down at the tiny ID photo of my mom affixed to one of her file documents. Even upside down she was lovely, exactly like all the photos I'd seen with her holding Duke's hand in her black tank suit or sitting on a bench by the lake in Lausanne, and, after Duke's early death, with her mom, Hedda, wearing her pretty dress, white stockings, an old-fashioned parasol by her knee. How different her youth was going to be this time around.

"I'll punish her, I swear to you. This kind of behavior is completely unacceptable. I don't know what my Republican cousin taught her about respecting diversity but things are going to be different from now on. Very different."

"Helen will develop respect, academic rigor and extracurricular interests soon," Gibson said. "That's what Bentwood is all about. Besides she must be in the middle of a difficult grief and adjustment process for both of you. You're suddenly a single mom."

"You're right," I said. "I guess I'm just worried that she'll turn out like so many girls today, only interested in looks and money."

"And then there's the turtle that's gone missing from the biology lab."

"Turtle?" I said. "You're kidding." This was too much. Had Mom really done all this in her first month? Was Bentwood targeting her for being different?

"A few days before Mr. Toots, the class mascot, disappeared, Helen asked if we could dissect him. The teacher explained that we don't dissect living turtles. Then, he was gone. I'm not accusing her of course, but I'm asking you to keep your eyes open. Helen might be acting out some adjustment issues."

"She may be, Mr. Gibson," I said, "but she isn't the type who needs to steal a turtle. We have plenty of money to go to the pet store. You'll have to back up this allegation with some proof."

"We try to instill strong values through volunteer projects as well as the study of urban literature and the history of labor movements," Gibson continued as if I hadn't said anything. "Be patient with her. Empathy doesn't happen overnight."

We stood up and I reached out to shake his hand. No wedding ring. Probably gay, like David.

"Oh, one more thing," he said. "I think she may also be having some father issues. You said hers was recently killed in a car accident."

I couldn't remember what the hell I'd told him.

"Yes," I said.

"Well, Mr. Edwards, our semi-retired part-time geography teacher, told me Helen stayed after class yesterday and asked him out for gelato."

"What?" I said. "Like on a date?"

Mr. Gibson smiled at me indulgently.

"He's an extremely dapper and charming older man but we discourage student teacher alliances for obvious reasons. And he is, after all, fifty years older than she is."

"Oh my goodness," I said. I had to sit down again.

Gibson patted me on the back.

"Don't take it too seriously, Ms. Pruitt."

"Call me Elizabeth," I said. "And I promise you won't see me in here again after I get through disciplining Helen. "

"I hope I do see you again," Jim said, leaving his hand on my back. "Call me Jim."

Maybe Mr. Edwards just misunderstood the friendly gesture of a young child."

"That's a possibility," he said, removing his hand. "My advice is to encourage her friendships with people her own age."

I stood up again.

"I will," I said. "Absolutely. Anything else?"

"You want to go out to dinner sometime?" he said.

"Jim," I said. "Are you kidding? Now you're asking me out on a date?"

"Actually, yes. Am I being too forward? Do you have a boyfriend?"

"How do I put this? Of the two genders, yours isn't my favorite one to date."

"Oh my," he said.

This time he sat down, looking blanched.

"Nothing personal," I said. "I think you're probably a fun guy and you're good looking too. It's just that in these cases, which I admit, given my robust stature and forthright manner, don't happen all that often, I think it's good to be blunt."

He opened his mouth but he couldn't seem to think of anything to say.

I had to let myself out of his office.

When I got home to Helen, I mentioned about the geography teacher and ignored the other discipline issues completely. The old man date was definitely the most awkward of all the infractions.

"Sometimes I forget how old I am," she said. "I couldn't help it. He is so cute."

"He's sixty or seventy years old, Helen."

"Well I know that. Give me a break. I'll adjust my libido downwards, OK?"

I poured both of us a glass of wine. That's the thing. Mom was two ages at once and we both knew it. I couldn't pretend she was a kid any more than I could imagine myself disciplining her for bad behavior, at least not for long.

We put our legs up on the mahogany coffee table I'd rescued from her beach house, channel surfed and ate a pepperoni pizza. In the middle of a two-part *Glee*, in spite of all the bad Helen-being-Helen behavior at Bentwood, I was having such a good time I wondered how could things have gotten any better.

During a long commercial break, Minerva called to ask how Helen's "trouble," as she called it, had gone at school. Kendra must have told her all about it. I decided, then and there, that Min was the kind of woman who, in order to get all the information, was only pretending to commiserate.

I was damned if I was going to let her pull me in again.

I said Helen and I had worked it all out and that the principal, Mr. Jim Gibson, was definitely interested in a date with me.

"Funny," Minerva said. "I always thought he was gay."

"Oh well," I said. "At least one of the three of us is."

"Could you get off that old record please?" she said. "You're the one who dumped me, if you'd care to recall."

Had I? I couldn't remember.

"I've got to go," I said.

"What are you watching?"

"Are you lonely? Where's Frank?"

"I'm just being friendly. I care about you. This reminds me how you never could make casual conversation."

That was a laugh. All I remembered about talking with Min was everything had to be about how we felt. How are you? You love me? What are you thinking about?

"We're reading, actually." Luckily the TV volume was on mute. "I'm re-reading *Emma* and Helen is annotating *Daisy Miller* just for fun."

She didn't have anything to say after that.

The next day when Helen brought Kendra home after school I thought I was going to burst. Their relationship had definitely risen to a new level. Remember that Mom had been the kind of citizen who voted conservative no matter who was running; the more the candidates slammed immigrants and welfare fraud, the more they looked liked her dear old dad, a southern gentleman and grandson of an honest-to-god Kentucky plantation owner, the better.

Her whole family believed African Americans were somehow less than human, sort of scary and had an odd smell. Acrid and peppery. That's actually what Mom had told me once.

But Mom's racism and conservative bent weren't across the board. While she had loved Ronald Reagan and Gerald Ford, Nixon left her cold. Plus, she thought Pat's pastel shirtwaist dresses made her look too much like a poor girl from the midwest. Of course she thought Jack and Jackie were fakes and hypocrites, hoarding their millions while spouting liberal slogans, but Mom did grudgingly admire them for their style and brains. Still none of this challenged her allegiance to the GOP.

"I'm not voting for their charisma like some idiots do," she'd always explained. "I'm not voting for their wives. I'm voting to conserve my way of life. That's what democracy is all about."

"So, Kendra's helping me with math and science," she said when they stopped in the kitchen to say hello.

"And Helen is helping me with social studies and creative writing. Together we make a perfect student."

"Very clever," I said. "No cheating going on, I hope."

"This is a time-honored practice," Helen said. "Girls studying together."

"We won't do each other's homework," Kendra said. "We just help."

I beamed at the two of them and gestured toward the kitchen. "I made banana pudding," I said. "Help yourselves."

Helen served Kendra a bowl of pudding and then scooped a big one for herself. I watched them leave, black and white, holding their snacks in one hand and their schoolbooks in another. I was happy again. Maybe Kendra would lead the way to the heights of liberal empathy I couldn't.

Later, when I heard them giggling, I peeked in to Helen's bedroom to watch. Was it too pathetic that I wished I could hang out there with them, maybe lounge on the bed and read magazines while they worked?

They were sitting side by side at the desk, their heads bent over a picture book about India. What was funny about India? The way the people worshipped cows?

"Elizabeth," Helen called out. We were a modern duo; she was permitted to call me, her cousin, by my first name.

"Yes," I said, leaning in as if I'd just been walking by.

"Fantastic pudding. Where'd you learn to cook like that?" she said. Not a question any real kid would ask an adult but still OK because Helen was officially from Iceland. Things were different there.

"I followed a recipe, honey," I said. "Thank you for such a nice compliment."

"You're welcome," she said.

"Come for dinner next weekend, Kendra," I said. "What do you like to eat?"

"I'm a vegetarian," she said.

"Wow," I said. "I've never heard that from somebody so young."

"Mexican," Kendra said. "Or pasta. That would be great. My stepmother never cooks."

"She doesn't?" I said.

I couldn't believe it. All she did when we were together was ask me if I wanted curried chicken or ratatouile or Belgian waffles. Probably she wanted to keep me fat so she'd look good in contrast.

I looked at Helen significantly to remind her how lucky she was to have me. Tonight I would cook from scratch. Rack of lamb, mint sauce and grilled baby red potatoes. Peas with a little sugar and lots of butter. Mom never had liked vegetables.

After dinner, as usual, I asked what she wanted to watch. As usual, we ate bowls of ice cream and after that I did her homework with one eye on the tube. If I didn't think about the ethics too hard, doing Helen's multiplication tables and vocabulary drills was kind of fun, like knitting.

Tonight we watched a made-for-TV drama about a young lesbian minister, played by Reece Witherspoon, of all people.

The movie conflict was inner and outer; could Reece stay in the church while facing all the misogyny and homophobia swirling around her?

"I'm distracted by her underbite," Helen said, dropping a bit of chocolate on her pretty white cotton nightie. She wiped it off with her napkin. "Don't forget the bleach when you wash it."

"How do you know about bleach? When did you ever load a washing machine?"

"How do you know if you're a lesbian?" she asked me back.

And in a bright flash of insight I remembered her head leaning close to Kendra's during the study session the night before. Their giggling at the sacred cows of India. Given my mother's "real" age, could this friendship be considered pedophilia?

I muted the volume on Reece, just now meeting her love interest, an atheist architect played by Natalie Portman.

"Helen," I said to her, "You just know."

"Oh," she said.

"Are you having feelings for Kendra?"

"I don't have feelings for Kendra," she said. "Can you turn the sound back on?"

"It's OK if you do. Nothing to be ashamed of."

"How can you stand it?" she said. "I gag at the thought."

"Stand what?"

"Touching a woman that way," she said. Her eyes wandered back to the television. She was already losing interest in my sexuality, which was just fine.

"I don't know," I said. "It's not something you can explain."

"I won't have grandchildren," she said halfheartedly.

"You don't like children," I said.

"Oh," she said.

"Besides, we could adopt," I said off the top of my head.

"Forget it," Helen said. "And change the channel. I don't want to think about lesbians anymore."

NINE

◆

A few months later, after dropping Helen off at Bentwood, I called David at Stillwaters. The truth is I was lonely for someone to talk to about Helen. I'd cut Doreen out of our lives and Minerva was in the dark about the reanimation. Obviously, Jim Gibson was out and after Mom officially died, I'd terminated with that therapist I'd seen for awhile.

The reason I'd stopped going was that bringing Mom back seemed too morally and emotionally fraught to explore with a therapist. In other words, if she'd actually believed me, I was pretty sure she would have tried to talk me out of it. Particularly after my lame suicide attempt.

What had I been thinking when I looked at those newborns in the hospital anyway?

Obviously, I couldn't really afford to be too introspective at this juncture in my life, but I could use some advice.

So that left David, the nice guy reanimation expert with the still frozen boyfriend.

"Hey," I said when he picked up. "It's Elizabeth. Remember me?"

"What's wrong?" he said, sounding harried.

"Well hello to you, too."

"Sorry," he said. "I'm just short staffed this morning. That horrible stomach flu is going around."

"I'll call back another time," I said. I'd pulled over near Helen's school so I could concentrate on talking.

"No, no," he said.

"I'm just needing to talk to somebody who understands about Mom."

And then, for god's sake, I started to cry.

"Now, now," David said. "If you get us sandwiches, I'll meet you in the park. You know, the one with the twisty slides and the artificial stream?"

"Noon?"

"OK," he said, "I have an hour." And then without saying goodbye he hung up.

I got us turkey sandwiches on wheat and drove to the park to wait. I spent part of the time watching ducks floating in the pond and people flying kites.

I opened up the copy of *National Enquirer* I'd picked up at the market and read about some other baseball player who'd had himself frozen after death. It was presented as fact, but like all those tabloid articles, it came across as fiction.

"Soon, soon," the spokeswoman for another cryonics company said. "We'll be bringing all our clients back within the next ten years."

And then there were photos of a shiny warehouse filled top to bottom with freezer compartments.

I turned to the article on Whitney Houston. I hoped that somebody had frozen her.

"Hi," David said. I jumped.

I patted the seat next to me and gave him his sandwich.

"I'm starving," he said. "What's up?"

"Mom's still pretty much a selfish bitch," I said.

I watched him while he chewed. He was a burly blond man, not your typical gay guy at all. In fact I wouldn't have picked him out in a million years on the street. Goes to show you.

"Oh well," he said. "At least you've got some money."

This conversation was so not working out.

"But am I going to learn anything from this? Is Mom?"

"That's up to you," David said, cryptically.

I gave up that line of conversation. Who did I think he was? Clearly not my new shrink.

"What about Raoul?" I said.

He choked on his last bite.

I pounded him on the back.

"Sorry," I said. I put my hand on his arm.

I felt like David and I were friends, but the truth was I didn't really know much about him. It was more like I was so desperate for a reanimation buddy, I'd manufactured a connection in my own head.

Silently we watched two little kids fight over a big red ball.

"I'm afraid," he whispered finally.

I took his big hand in mine. It was forward, but with both of us being gay, for some reason I figured it was OK.

"Go on," I said.

"I'm afraid of what might happen between us if I do. That he might not love me anymore."

"Keep talking," I said, like a good therapist, the kind who doesn't judge.

"I like the control I have now. I can talk to him and he doesn't talk back. I can pull out his drawer at will."

"You can even control the sex, can't you?"

"How do you know about that?" he said, reddening.

"Just a guess," I said. "No big deal. Everybody's got some weird shit they do in secret. It's called being human."

"Don't think I'm a necrophiliac," he said. "It's much more complicated than that."

And then David began to sob, probably from the relief of letting it all out finally, the shame, the need, the grief.

"What else?" I said. I took a bite of my sandwich and remembered that I'd originally intended this meeting to be all about me and Mom. It was feeling so good to be able to draw him out I began to think I could have been a therapist myself. I suddenly understood why people become shrinks. You get to forget about your problems and be your best self even if you have to pretend.

"I was always afraid of Raoul leaving me," David continued. "When he stayed for five years I didn't think, here's proof I can trust him. I only thought, I'm five years closer to his running away. And then he got sick and I took care of him. By that time he needed me too much to leave."

For a while we listened to the birds and kids and cars.

"I've never told anybody that," he said.

"Wow," I said. "Thanks."

So, almost a year to the day after we had that conversation, when David called and invited me and Helen to Stillwaters for Raoul's reanimation ceremony, I was so excited I almost burst.

Nothing much had changed between me and Helen, except we had gotten used to our relationship. There was less stress but not much affection.

Still, soon there would be another one like Helen even if he were several decades older in body.

"We're the only guests," I said.

"Big deal," Helen said. "I don't want to go."

"Why not?" I said. I was brushing her thick brown hair, like a medieval maid, counting the strokes under my breath. After a year and a half together, it was the only physical thing she'd let me do.

"Boring," she said.

But, über therapist that I'd become, I read her like a book.

"You just don't want to think of yourself that way," I said.

"Ouch," she said, grabbing the brush out of my hand. "What way?"

"Reanimated. Undead."

"That's mean," she said and began to pull the loose strands from the bristles. "Here," she said and handed the hairball to me.

"I'm supposed to save this?"

"No," she giggled. "Not unless you want to. Throw it in the wastebasket."

But I got her to go with me to Stillwaters the best way I knew how. Her way. Bribery. I told her I'd get her a new sweater if she joined me for the ceremony.

"It won't be a long service," I said. "Just give them these."

I handed her a bouquet I'd put in a glass vase I'd picked up from her old house.

A half an hour later, I dragged her into the waiting room. We sat there for an unusually long time, listening to strange sounds of shouting and crashing.

"Let's go," Helen said, trying to wiggle out of my grip.

Finally David came in to talk to us. He was holding a handkerchief over a bloody nose.

"Go home," he said. "It's not safe here. I'm cancelling the festivities."

Then Raoul dove past him, buck naked, equipped like a stallion. He was chased by a couple of nurses whom David waved back.

"Wow," Helen said, checking him out. "You have a great body, young man."

Raoul stopped in his tracks. He took her hand and kissed it. "Thank you, young lady," he said. "You can imagine my shock at returning so old."

And that's when I remembered about David's plan to age progress his boyfriend for the good of their relationship.

"You're not old at all," she said. "I would have given anything to have had a boyfriend like you."

"This is Helen," David said. "She's reanimated like you."

"How old were you when you died?" Raoul asked.

"Never mind," David said, evidently covering up her deep age regression.

"We wanted to thank you again," Mom said. "We are so happy with your work."

There was a long silence while she tried to get another glimpse of Raoul's penis, by now hidden away under a towel he'd draped over himself.

"Thank you, Helen," David said. "You've been just what the doctor ordered. Come on, baby," he said to Raoul. "Let's go put on some clothes."

"I know what he's been doing," David said to me a month or so later. We were sitting at Aquarium in the patio, next to a pond holding the pretty non-edibles, like goldfish and koi.

I had plenty of free time to go out to lunch now that I didn't need to work. What with raising Helen and all the money we had, I'd given my housecleaning business away to my best employee, Claudia. We signed all the papers in front of a bi-lingual lawyer and at the last minute I'd added this clause: "If you don't make a profit, you have to give the business back."

Claudia said she'd always do my house for free.

"I know it's a male gay cliché but it's the truth," David went on. "Raoul's having sex with anybody he can."

"How do you know that?"

"He told me, for god's sake. He describes the details. And I listen. Like we're friends or it turns me on."

"Does it?"

"What's that got to do with it? You lesbians don't understand a thing."

"Kick him out."

"I love him."

Suddenly I remembered exactly what had happened with Min, why we broke up. We'd been lying in bed together on a Sunday morning when, out of the blue, she told me she loved me.

Usually when she said tried to say stuff like that, I'd discourage her by rolling my eyes and yawning.

This time I asked her why she was telling me that now, as if she was covering up something bad.

"You had a dream about sex with somebody else," I'd said.

Min burst into tears.

I remained stolid.

She bit my shoulder.

I pushed her off the bed.

It was embarrassing to remember it all now. No wonder it had taken me so long.

"Oh, Elizabeth, you are so crazy," she'd said. "I tell you I love you and you insist on the opposite. It's all because of that mother of yours. You think everybody doesn't love you."

Then she'd climbed back up into bed and kissed me that sweet way she had, all over my face and then down the center of my body, saying tender soft words at each stop.

But instead of enjoying it, I kept on. Sometimes with lovers, I had a demon inside me, itchy and hot.

"You dreamed about sex with a man, didn't you? You can't stand me because I don't have a penis." On and on I went with that stuff at poor Min, louder, until I finally forced her all the way out the bedroom door and into her car. And then I wouldn't let her back in until she promised to move out for good.

And then she found herself a man almost as if she was doing it for me.

"Well, then accept the suffering if you're so desperate to hang on to him," I said to David now. "He should be grateful."

"Do you think Helen's grateful?"

"That level of emotion isn't really in her character. She's much more concrete. Ask about hungry or greedy."

"You know a good therapist, Elizabeth?" David said.

We were eating sushi, a recent addition to the menu on account of the death and reanimation of a gifted sushi chef from Tokyo. He'd been traveling in the U.S. when he was poisoned by an incorrectly cleaned pufferfish.

An ugly and ironic death. But at least we knew that the sushi would be safe at Aquarium.

"Raoul can't go to therapy; you know that," I said. "He and Mom can't tell the truth about their lives, where they're from. Let's just hope he'll calm down after awhile. Or else he'll die from his recklessness. Although that doesn't do you much good."

It felt like I was talking about an un-neutered Boxer.

"I've wondered something," David said between sips of his miso soup.

"What?"

"If this extreme behavior might be a result of age manipulation."

"Helen isn't extreme," I said. "She's just Helen."

As soon as I said it, I could feel the denial.

"Great," he said snidely. "So things are working out perfectly for you."

"She's still breaking the rules at school. Things aren't perfect. Just predictable."

"She and Raoul should get together and have a talk."

"Why?" I said. "So they can egg each other on with better ideas of how to torture us?"

"Oh come on," he said. "How much worse could they get?"

So the next weekend here they were standing at the front door, holding a yellow balloon with "Happy Independence Day" printed on the front. It was early July but not that kind of party. Luckily Helen didn't care.

She ran to take it from David and hug him around the waist. She had turned into a big hugger particularly if you brought her a present or gave her back her entire youth.

"It's all we could find at the market," Raoul said. "Not as nice as the flowers you brought to my reanimation, but better than nothing."

When we got inside we all took a long look at him, this time clothed.

He was wearing a white linen plantation suit and a dapper straw hat, as if he was Cuban aristocracy from a hundred years ago. His skin was brown and warm and he was sporting a small mustache.

"Last time we saw you your private parts were flying around," she said.

"Now you look like a cigar baron," I said. "Wow."

"You are so handsome," she said. "What I want to know is why you didn't come back young like me?"

David and I gasped. Maybe this get-together wasn't such a good idea after all.

"Because David wanted me old."

"Oh honey, we've talked about this," David said. "Reanimation is an inexact science. Besides, you're distinguished. Maturity is sexy."

"Helen," I said. "Bring in the champagne, would you?"

"Son of a bitch," Raoul said. "Tell her the truth. You wanted to make me ugly so you'd have me all to yourself."

After a few more minutes of the boys' bickering, Helen tottered back in on the high heels she'd insisted on wearing, carrying champagne and four flutes. She was just in time. It was obvious that David and Raoul were still having big trouble.

She was also wearing tight jeans and a t-shirt reading 'Princess of the World' which revealed the outline of her budding breasts. I could see Raoul watching her, comparing himself with bitterness. This get-together was turning into a terrible mistake.

We carried our drinks out onto the deck where luckily things got a little better.

She took a big sip of champagne.

"I'm glad to see you let her drink," Raoul said, lighting a big cigar.

"Why?" I said.

"Well, it's obvious," he said, blowing several excellent smoke rings. "She's going to need some relief. The wisdom of a 70 year old woman trapped in the succulent body of a young girl would drive anybody crazy."

"Thanks for understanding, Raoul," Helen said, topping off her flute with the pretty pink bubbly. "Elizabeth doesn't, of course. I'm actually back to look for some good loving. When I was seventeen, my boyfriend left me after my father killed himself. There was a scandal and the boy's parents made him go."

Then she began to whimper a little bit, rubbing her eyes until they were red and puckering her lips so they quivered like a babe.

"Poor Mom," I said. "She lost everything at once."

"And my Daddy too. He really loved me."

Hearing her explain her reanimation motivation in front of David and Raoul had a strong positive effect on me, almost as if I'd never heard it before. No wonder she'd been such an awful mother. No wonder she'd lost all her ability for empathy and love. Only money and objects matter once you lose everything else.

On the other hand, once again, she'd forgotten to mention me.

"I never got over him," she added quietly, playing it up big for Raoul.

"I know exactly what you mean," he said, taking her hand in his.

They were totally hitting it off. I remembered that Mom had been a good fag hag the first time around too, sharing intimacies with the hairdresser and the gem queen who sold her big emerald rings she didn't need. After she died, I sold all of them back to him, at a loss.

"Want to see my bedroom?" she said to Raoul.

"Everything," he said. "I may be a promiscuous old homosexual, but I love young ladies. Their smooth skin, their glossy hair, the smell of their pink shell ears."

"Are they safe together?" I asked David after they left.

"I don't know," he said, looking gray. "He's never talked like this before. I don't understand him anymore. He wants to hurt me for some reason."

"Maybe you shouldn't have manipulated his age, David. That might have been going too far."

"Are you saying I was acting too much like a gay god?"

"Well, not that I believe that God has a gender or sexual preference, but yes, exactly."

That got him to laugh.

"Should we go listen at the door?" he said.

"Sure, what do we have to lose?"

We crouched behind a bookcase and tried to hold our breath so we could hear what Raoul and Helen were saying to each other. We definitely had a lot to lose.

"You are so delicious. Let me see your chest."

"I thought you were gay, not a pedophile."

"This is for research purposes."

"OK, but only if you show me your wee-wee."

"I thought you saw it already."

"I want to see it again."

Long silence.

"Look how perky your tits are. My balls are already starting to droop."

Long silence.

"You're right, although I haven't seen any in years."

"See what he did to me. I have to pay for a blowjob. Who would want me now?"

"Try being thirteen. I can't do a thing. I have no money. I have to go to stupid school. It's driving me crazy. I feel like I'm going to explode."

"Maybe I can help with that. Sit."

Long silence. They must have been on the Internet.

"Maybe we shouldn't listen," David whispered. There were tears in his eyes.

"Oh, lifeguards," Helen squealed. "I've always loved them so much."

"Me too," Raoul said. Then the slap of a high five.

Long silence. Poor David sat down on the floor and put his head in his hands.

Sound of shuffling in the closet.

"Where the hell did you get that?" Raoul said, this time his voice sounding high- pitched and freaked. "Be careful, Helen. Don't you come near me with it."

God, I wanted to storm the bedroom. David gripped my ankle just in case.

"This one loves mice and kittens," she giggled.

"Does she know you have that thing?"

"Oh, Elizabeth doesn't have a clue. There are a lot of things she doesn't know. I think she might still be a virgin."

"David told me she's a lesbian."

"Whatever," she said.

That's when David and I stopped listening and returned to the back yard where we drank the rest of the champagne in silence.

Finally David repeated his favorite phrase, "Reanimation's not an exact science."

I said, "And neither is love."

TEN

That evening Helen was full of something resembling affection, but I didn't buy it. She and Raoul had probably made a pact to be nice to us, their benefactors, at least until they didn't need us around anymore. How sad a thought was that?

And what was the secret she had in her bedroom? I made a plan to check it out when she was at school tomorrow.

I was beginning to believe she and Raoul were handsome aliens, not-quite-human similacrums of our loved ones. For some reason, that idea gave me comfort.

"You're thinking I should help with the housework more?" she said, painting her nails while I did the dinner dishes.

Avatars could read your mind, couldn't they?

"That would be nice," I said. "It would be nice if you offered. That would show something."

"I wonder if we could hire me a personal manicurist like I used to have?" she said. "I'm not very good at this."

She showed me her nails, which did indeed look pretty ragged.

"Mom," I said, scrubbing my last pan, "things aren't like that any more. You're supposed to be a regular kid. We can make an appointment at a beauty salon if you want your nails done."

I couldn't remember if I'd ever seen a thirteen year old at my place, Cuts and Curls.

"I'm not a regular kid," she said. "We both know that."

Now she was painting her thumbnails black and trying to stick little pink stars in the center. It kind of broke my heart.

"You're right," I said. "It's just that I thought this time..."

"You brought me back so you could change me, didn't you, Elizabeth?" she interrupted. "The truth is you don't like me very much. You never have. Me and my car detailers and manicurists."

"Did you get this idea from Raoul?"

One of her old Waterford champagne flutes slipped out of my hands. It shattered all over the place.

She laughed.

"You think I need some old queen to help me figure you out?"

"Well," I said. "Let's put it this way. I'd hoped to give you a variety of new experiences to try."

"Broaden my horizons? I'm the same person inside that I always was. Can't you tell?"

"I'll have to sweep this up," I said. "I'm sorry I broke your glass."

I hated my compulsion to apologize to her. She didn't care about the glass any more than I did. Why was I still saying, "please love me, Mom. Don't be mad," like it mattered?

She blew on her nails.

"You could hire Doreen to help out if you're tired of the housework. I'm sure she could use the money."

"You've been talking to her?"

"She called me for a reference."

Another secret. Helen was full of them.

"You're dead," I said. "How can you give her a reference?"

"I am not dead, god dammit. I was frozen, then I was unfrozen."

I got down on my hands and knees to sweep up the glass.

"Ah, Mom," I said, emptying the dustpan. "I adore you. I always have. Surely you know that."

"You'd better," she said, glaring at me.

It was a little scary, having her see right into me that way. When I knew her before, she only looked in my direction and maybe through me to the other side.

Was this better?

"The only tough thing is that I'm jealous of your smooth skin and all those delightful years you have ahead of you, all that hope and surprise."

"And drinking and smoking and sex," she giggled.

I looked out the kitchen window, but all I could see was my own reflection. A soft, sad middle-aged woman with doom written all over her face.

"What's wrong with you?" Helen said. But before she could read my mind again there was a sharp knock on the kitchen door. We both jumped.

"Who's there?" I said. I was a little bit wary. It was 10:30 at night.

Helen peaked through the blinds.

"Maria Garcia," the voice said. "Your neighbor."

I opened the door.

FROZEN

:ia stood there shivering, her face all lit up by the porch light. I could see that she'd been crying. She was tall and hip, a younger Joan Baez, with long salt and pepper hair hanging over her shoulders and loads of silver bracelets flowing up her wrists.

"Come in," I said.

"No," she said. "It's late. I just came to check if you'd seen Pablo. I've been calling and calling all night and I saw that your light was on."

"Who?" Helen said in a snotty voice.

"Pablo," Maria said louder, "my cat."

Helen snickered behind her black and pink nails.

"No," I said. "I'm sorry, Maria. I haven't seen him at all. I'm sure he'll be back soon."

I turned to close the door but she didn't move.

"Ask her," she said, looking at Helen.

"Helen?" I said.

"Nope," she said. "Not hide nor hair."

Maria watched her suspiciously.

"I've seen her walking out at night," Maria said. "With a flashlight."

"Like the border patrol?" Helen said, smirking at her.

"Watch her," Maria said ominously and left.

"She's jealous," Helen said after the door closed, "because I'm young and more beautiful than she is. Plus I have white skin. That's why she wears so much silver, so she'll reflect the light like the moon. All dark people want to be light. Kendra told me that. I'm not making it up."

"Whatever," she said.

"What do you know about the cat? What did you show Raoul? You're keeping secrets from me."

"That woman sniffs cocaine with her son."

I closed the dishwasher and turned it on.

"Stop doing whatever you're doing," I said trying to sound authoritative but actually feeling tragic impotence. "Or else."

"Or else?" she laughed. "I'm not listening to you anymore. I have better things to do."

Just then I heard a cat scream. Or it could have been a small child.

"Gotta go," she said, ran down the hall and slammed her bedroom door.

I stayed in the kitchen and put my hands over my ears. For a while that seemed to work. Then it didn't.

I tried to get into her room but she'd locked it. I pounded as hard as I could. Then I bounced my shoulder against it a few times. Finally it opened.

And what I saw then I'll never forget.

Helen dangling the cat, Pablo, above a python's mouth, teasing the snake, torturing the cat. This must have been what had scared Raoul earlier; Helen had freaked him with her enormous killer reptile.

"Stop it, Helen," I shouted, pulling the cat out of her hands. Most of the python was still coiled on the floor in some sort of cage.

"Ouch. Damn cat scratched me," she said grabbing back.

Then I did what I had to do. I pushed her onto the bed and then tossed the cat out her open window so it could make a dash for home.

Helen looked at me like she didn't know who I was and then, after that, with something like respect.

Pushing her as hard as I did wasn't as difficult for me as you might think. In fact it was sort of exhilarating. In fact, it felt so great I wanted to run a marathon. I'd just saved a cat's life from my mom.

I handed her a towel to stop the bleeding from a cut above her eyebrow where my ring must have nicked her skin.

"You hit me," she said, touching the blood. "I can't believe it. You abused me."

"You're crazy, Helen. You were feeding a cat to a snake. Think about it."

She kicked the python cage shut and began to try excuses on me.

"I was simply playing in the wild animal kingdom. It's a natural impulse. It's a release of all the tension I carry inside. At my age there are millions of bad things kids do. It's better than if I was doing teenage drugs or sex. At least I'm not cutting myself or throwing up or bullying other girls."

"It's a natural impulse for animals, not little girls."

I remembered how she'd joked about Oscar, my pet crab when I was a kid.

"But you've always been a bit of an animal torturer, haven't you?" I went on. "It's an addiction, like that football player, Vick, with his dogs. Is Doreen your supplier? Does she buy you small animals to hurt and feed to the snake? Did you feed the python that turtle, Mr. Toots?"

Helen tried to smile but I could see she was worried about how much I knew.

"Take me to Emergency," she said, "before I bleed to death."

Most of the other people in Emergency at this hour looked dangerous and addicted, with big tattoos on their arms depicting objects of dread, swastikas or skulls. A few were tiny feverish babies and elderly folks who didn't know where the hell they were.

Helen didn't notice anything. She was pressing on her wound as if it was about to fly open.

"Alright. I feel bad," I said. "I shouldn't have hit you."

"There goes my old heart doctor," she whispered as a skinny rabbit-y guy hurried through. "I wonder what he's doing here at this hour?"

"Maybe he got demoted after you died," I said. "As a punishment."

"Doctor Williams," she called out. I put my hand over her mouth.

"Who were you going to tell him you are?"

She yanked my hand off her face and looked around her. She'd been in the emergency room lots of times with Doreen. I'd even taken her myself once on Christmas Eve for an ingrown toenail.

"I want you to know I'm missing a big party at Kendra's right now," Helen said.

"It's next week," I said. I knew because Minerva had asked me to help chaperone.

"How can I go with a horrible gash on my forehead?"

"We'll comb your hair to cover it," I said. I was feeling guilty but not too much. Was that progress?

"That baby over there is dripping snot all over his mother's hand," she said. "Disgusting."

"I know," I said.

"And that old man has a big wet stain between his legs. People should be put out of their misery before they get like that. I hate this place."

"Ms. Pruitt," a nurse said finally.

"That's you and me," I said.

We went in to a curtained cubicle where the nurse took a look at her cut and winced.

"You're a brave girl," she said.

On cue, Helen smiled bravely, her lips quivering slightly. And, watching that, damn if I wasn't back to loving her as much as ever. She was so cute and strong. Mom was an addiction, pure and simple. A mother-love habit I couldn't seem to break.

Soon the doctor came, but it wasn't really necessary. The nurse had already put a butterfly bandage over the cut.

"Looks good, Shari," the doctor said. She was a small Indian-looking gal with a diamond stud in her nose, the kind of free spirit who liked working ER.

She sat down in the extra chair and took turns looking at both of us.

"Who did this to you?" she said to Helen. "I have to make a report."

"I'll tell you what happened," she said. "She did…"

Mom was excited the way she always got when someone showed an interest. It hadn't occurred to her that the real story might break up our happy home.

I couldn't help it. I began to cry.

Mom stopped for a moment and reconsidered.

"Go on," the doctor said, twisting the diamond. "Would you like your mother to leave so we can have some privacy?"

"She did the best she could to catch me," she said. "I fell against my dresser. We were playing with the cat."

"Are you sure?" the doctor said.

"Yes," Helen said. "But she's not my mother. I'm her mother."

"Whoa," the doc said. "Maybe we need to do a brain scan."

"Just kidding," she said, collecting herself. "Let's go. No scar I hope."

"Here's a hotline number," the doctor said, handing her a help line card.

On the way out to the car, Helen unaccountably took my hand.

"I'm staying home from school tomorrow. We'll have a mani and a pedi. You'll make my favorite spaghetti."

She was blackmailing me again of course. But this time it felt pleasantly familiar, like an old blanket when you're all alone.

"I'm so sorry," I said as we got into the car.

"I forgive you," she said. "Just stop crying."

We drove home by way of the gelato place that was open late. Helen was happily talking nonstop, but I was so shaken up by both the snake and the slap, I almost rear-ended a couple of cars. She didn't notice.

ELEVEN

◆

The next day, responding immediately to Helen's pressure, I took us to the fanciest spa in town. It wasn't exactly appropriate for kids, particularly in the bathing suit optional Roman Jacuzzi, but since it was a weekday, I figured not too many customers would be around.

"Did my breasts sag that much?" Helen whispered over the sound of jets and piped in Vivaldi. A perfectly average middle-aged woman was climbing into the marble tub across from us. Helen had insisted on showing off her naked budding body to the three or four others in the water, which meant that I had to go in naked as well.

"No," I said automatically. "But you did have open wounds on your legs frequently, so you wouldn't have been allowed to hang out here."

She positioned her back against a jet.

"Hey, Elizabeth, this feels great." Her eyes closed with pleasure. It occurred to me that maybe she was using the water to stimulate herself.

I looked away.

After toweling off, we were led to our treatment room, a musky space with the requisite candles and tinkly instrumental music. We were having the couples' massage, which the spa had suggested, given Helen's age, so she wouldn't be by herself.

Lying on our backs with two young women kneading our feet and calves, I listened to Mom tell more stories of her life. My slugging her in the face the day before seemed to loosen her up.

"My father held my hand over a lighted candle at dinner when I refused to eat those sweetbreads the cook loved to serve."

"How long?"

"Until my mother could smell the burning flesh."

"He was an angry man. Poor you."

"Why do you say that?" she said, kicking her foot out of the masseuse's hand.

"Sorry, sorry," the gal said.

"Too hard," Helen said.

I could tell she was still completely in love with my grandfather, who, consumed by his own demons, left her behind too young to ever grow up. It was a lot like I still felt about her, my sadistic, self-centered mother, except that she hadn't left me behind.

Just the opposite.

My technician was doing my hands with great skill. I sighed with pleasure. I was clearly the easier client.

"One time," Helen continued, "he stood at the end of my mother's bed in the middle of the night with a gun in his hand. She left him after that and moved us in with her parents. I never saw him again."

"She had to leave, Helen," I said. "He needed psychological help and medication."

"She drove him to it," she said.

I'd always noticed that Helen had an answer for everything. Everything was black and white no matter how complex the situation or the people. I made a silent vow to try to be more like her that way, loving objects and old memories, simple solutions and clichés. It seemed so much easier.

I knew inside it was impossible. Mom and I had never been anything alike. In fact, more and more I was realizing we were almost the complete opposite, which made things like trying to understand each other pointless. How sad was that? And how confusing.

"Cute girl except for this cut on her face," the girl at the main desk said as we paid, accepting the twenty-dollar tip I made Helen hand over for her masseuse. "Did you fall down?"

Helen waved her away.

"Some people are so nosy," she said when we got into the car.

"You can get your hair cut to cover it," I said.

"I want people to see it," she said. "What's the point of bruises and cuts unless people notice them?"

I swung into the driveway.

Maria Garcia waved at us from her front porch where she was petting big Pablo. As soon as he saw us, he bolted.

That night for dinner I ground up a big sleeping pill into Helen's mashed potatoes with gravy, her favorite, and after she fell asleep, I removed the python. I drove him in his cage to the woods at the edge of town. I put the cage on the ground, quickly opened the latch and ran back to the car. It was probably an irresponsible release, leaving the big lug to fend for himself in the unfamiliar woods, but let somebody else deal with him. I had enough problems of my own.

TWELVE

◆

Things were pretty much the same for a few years after that. We shopped for skimpier clothes in bigger sizes; Helen tried marijuana and, with me doing all her math and science homework, we got all the way through sophomore year at Bentwood. Minerva and Kendra hung around and I pretended they were our great friends, shopping and traveling together sometimes. Minerva still got on my nerves but as long as she didn't keep telling me how much I meant to her, we managed OK.

David and Raoul stayed together too, mostly because David looked the other way and practically lived at his job. Raoul managed Aquarium when he wasn't running around with younger men and lifeguards.

I don't think Helen had had any sex yet.

Which didn't matter really, given the fact that David had assured me that all reanimateds were sterile. No risk of pregnancy or an ugly abortion.

"The older girls tell me what it's like now," she said one evening while we were watching *Sex in the City*. The masseuse at the television spa was giving Kim Cattrall's character, Samantha, a bonus, surprise cunnilingus.

"They do?" I said, mildly interested.

"It's much better than in my day, when most men didn't know women could have orgasms in the first place. Or didn't know what to do about it."

I still spent most of my time trying to keep Helen happy. I'd given up changing her character to get her to be a better person, but I did want to keep her with me as part of my life. Even with my whole soul being sacrificed on the altar of Mom, I still enjoyed her. I still loved her. I still needed her, truth be told.

We'd moved to a new neighborhood, a beautiful place overlooking the ocean, not too far from her old house, the one I'd sold after she died. I tried to fit in. I took tennis lessons at the club and walked dogs at the pet shelter.

I hadn't gotten us a dog for obvious reasons. Who knew how long she could keep herself from torturing the poor thing?

The house was even better than the old one and Helen was lovelier, if possible, than the first time she'd been sixteen, at least from the photographic evidence I'd saved. Maybe it was the higher quality of modern food or orthodontics. Or was it my good enough re-parenting? Who knew?

But the white-carpeted spread overlooking the dreamy indigo bay and her total fresh beauty evidently couldn't take the place of that boyfriend she'd come back to find. We both knew that Helen was determined to fall in love soon—the entire reason she'd returned to me.

I wanted her to be happy, but at the same time I didn't want her to screw up her second chance at life by getting a second-rate first boyfriend. I'd given up on changing her crappy right-wing values, but at least I wanted her to find somebody kind, somebody well-intentioned, somebody dull like my dad.

Or, like Kevin, the steady and adept after school bagger at the market. But when I whispered to Helen how careful he was with the eggs, she didn't even look up from her trashy tabloid article about LiLo looking wasted.

"How's your team doing this year?" I asked him. It was a sure-fire good question; wasn't every boy his age on some type of team?

"Oh for God's sake," Helen said, looking around at the other guys, "Let him do his job."

"The chess team made it to state playoffs," he smiled. "Thanks for asking."

"This is my cousin, Helen. I think you two might have a lot in common."

"What's *his* name?" she said, pointing at the Bad Boy bagger tossing things into somebody's cloth satchel at the "five items or less" aisle. His hiring was clearly the result of nepotism gone wild. He looked deeply unemployable: tattoos, earrings, spicky black hair. And scary too.

"Filippo," sweet Kevin said. "He's from New York. The manager's nephew."

I grabbed Helen with one hand and our bag with the other. She was panting like a dog in heat.

Finally, three months later, at the beginning of her junior year, she nabbed herself a first boyfriend, not a Bad Boy, but much worse. He was attractive and had a good job, but he had to be at least thirty years old. And he was married, to an actress, and a teacher at Bentwood. The drama coach, to be exact.

Can you get worse than that?

"This is Jeremy, my boyfriend," Helen said to me one day after school. I was sitting in the living room, reading the paper, waiting for her to report in, like any good guardian would. Mostly I picked her up, or Kendra, who had her license already, drove her home. But today she'd called to say she was going to get a ride with "somebody new." Thinking she'd meant a regular friend, I'd baked sugar cookies for the occasion.

Jeremy had curly black hair that kept falling over his eyes and something wrong with his right leg, which gave him the look of a youthful character in Somerset Maugham.

"You're so old," I said to him before I could stop. I stood up and gathered myself for this odd confrontation. I was taller by a few inches in my bare feet.

Jeremy reached out his hand.

"Nice to meet you too, ma'am," he said.

"How old are you anyway?" I said.

"Oh for god's sake, Elizabeth. Don't be a pill," Helen said. "I'm not in grade school anymore."

We sat down in the living room, Jeremy and Helen on the couch, me in a chair. When Jeremy put his arm over her shoulders, something rose up inside me, something dark and ugly I didn't know was there.

I realized two things: they'd had sex, probably lots of it and right now, this man owned her no matter what I did.

"I'm Helen's Cousin Elizabeth," I said. "But I guess you already figured that out."

Jeremy winked at me.

"Of course you are," he said.

Had Helen told him about being reanimated? I couldn't believe it.

He kissed her on the cheek.

She had.

"Could you point me to the rest room, Cousin Elizabeth?" Jeremy said.

"That way," I said, pointing towards the hall.

"Beautiful view," he said as he left.

Helen and I watched Jeremy dip and drag himself out of the room.

"Jeremy's my drama coach," she said. "I've told him everything about us. Stillwaters, cryonics, the whole nine yards."

I looked away abruptly. It was as if Helen had punched me in the chest. I didn't want her to see how bad it pained me.

"He helped me realize the depth I could bring to my roles, having lived one entire life already. He's very creative. In fact, I'd say he's brilliant. He studied theater at Oxford."

"You told him everything?" I said.

"This is what I came back for, Elizabeth. I can feel it. He's the soul mate I never had."

Neither Helen nor I had ever told anybody outside about the cryonics. It had been a silent pact between us. Now I felt like our only real bond was broken.

I covered my shock and disappointment the best way I knew how. Biting sarcasm.

"Monica Lewinsky's high school boyfriend was her drama coach too," I said as sarcastically as I could. "But he didn't have a limp."

"Car accident when he was a kid," Helen said. "And Monica Lewinsky was fat and pathetic, and that acting coach was just using her for sex. Jeremy wants to marry me when I get old enough. He happens to be married at the moment, but they're practically separated. She's an actress on TV, so she's away a lot. He wants to help me get an agent."

"Were you born yesterday?" I said. "Have you never heard of the casting couch? Or statutory rape? You're only approximately sixteen."

"Going on 75," she said. "Are you jealous? Why don't you like him? You've hardly spoken to him. Don't you like his voice?"

"His voice is irrelevant," I said, trying to stay cool. "I just think it shows a significant lack of character for an adult teacher to hit on a high school girl."

"You and I both know I'm not really a teen."

"You told him everything?" I said again.

"I sure did," she said. "You, reanimation, what I like to do in bed."

"You've had sex?"

"Why are you so upset?" she said. "It's not like I never had it before. And it sure is better this time around."

I didn't want to think about it.

"The reanimation's supposed to be a secret. We promised David. We could hurt Stillwaters if the details went public."

"Jeremy won't tell anybody," Helen said. "I trust him."

"Who else have you told?" I asked dejectedly.

"Nobody," she said. "Don't be so uptight."

"How long have you been having sex?"

"You really want to know?"

"No," I said.

If she'd been promiscuous, like Raoul, it wouldn't have been a surprise given her behavior the first time around.

When I was growing up, she and my dad never seemed to be in the same bed at the same time. For example, they'd rent a big house in Palm Springs for Easter break, stick me in the maid's room, and invite loads of friends to hang out by the pool. At night they'd all dance to Sinatra crooning over the loudspeakers. And even after half a dozen highballs, most of the guests still had the energy to fuck each other in all sorts of unlikely combinations.

I knew because, just like at the beach that time, I used to wander from room to room looking for my mom in the middle of the night.

"He's great at sex," Helen said. "The best I've ever had."

"I repeat, I don't want to hear about you and Jeremy in bed," I said.

I hated the drama teacher. I hated him because he was arrogant, an abuser of children and such a big threat to me. Selfish as she was, I had hoped to be with Mom for a while longer before she actually ran away with somebody else.

"He's been in the bathroom a long time," I said. "You sure he's not stealing the silver?"

"I told him to go to my bedroom afterwards. We're going to practice my lines. I'm the lead in a play he wrote for me himself." Helen smiled at me and got up to leave.

"Helen," I said. "Be careful."

It occurred to me that I should have been telling that to Jeremy instead.

THIRTEEN

◆

In spite of the fact that we both knew she wasn't really a teen, I quickly scheduled a meeting with Jeremy to threaten exposure of the affair. I told myself Helen was as vulnerable this time as she had been when she'd gotten dumped by Paul Robbins, the brute from sixty years before.

The boyfriend and I sat facing each other on the bare stage, and although he stared right past me, I refused to be unnerved. And while there was something deeply theatrical and tragic about the conversation, I kept reminding myself that he was only a high school acting coach, not Romeo or Othello or anybody like that.

"So you're an actor?" I said. "Have I seen you in anything?"

His eyes shifted.

"Theater mostly and a couple of commercials."

Bull's-eye.

"Nothing much then," I said.

Too bad I wasn't in control of the lighting. I could have stuck the spotlight right on his face.

"Teaching is satisfying work. It takes up a great deal of time to put on a show."

"And it gives you a perfect opportunity to prey on children," I said.

Jeremy answered predictably.

"Helen is no child."

"She's just sixteen. How dare you contradict me? I could get you thrown in jail. I could have the school closed."

"You won't," he said smoothly. "I know all about her history and I believe her. I did some serious reading in the field of cryonics and I see how it could work. Besides, nobody's that good an actress to be able to convince me if it wasn't the truth."

God I hated this man. I could, though, understand how he was so into my mom. In a flash of compassionate insight, I thought of Doreen and me and all her other groupies, and I understood Jeremy perfectly. Underneath all his thespian bravado, he loved his narcissists as much as the rest of us did.

As the kids walked in to set up for rehearsal, Jeremy continued with me.

"But, most importantly," he said, "I could, if I chose to, very convincingly expose what you've done to her, the mind control, the de facto imprisonment. So let's cool it with the intimidation and just go watch the rehearsal. I think you'll find Helen's acting remarkable."

"I've seen her act every day of my life."

"You are so bitter," Jeremy said condescendingly.

"Why are you betraying your wife and family, risking your career, your entire world for my mother?" I said to him after we moved to the front row of the auditorium. "Her personality will only get worse as the years go on. She will expect to be provided for in a grand fashion. She hates children. She will only come to feel contempt for you."

He sighed deeply, so bored.

I kept at him.

"You're a big fish in a small pond, Jeremy," I said. "High school drama coach. How silly is that?"

He looked at his nails.

"But then none of this matters, does it? You're not planning on a future with her. You're dallying with her while she's here at BHS. Unless you're stopped, you'll move on to the next young thing after she's gone."

"Listen to me, you wacko," Jeremy said finally, with surprising vehemence. "You're holding your own mother hostage. Don't you judge me. Don't you threaten me. Look to yourself, woman."

With a flourish, Jeremy turned and from his seat began to direct.

I knew I'd met my match. He may have been a high school drama coach, but Jeremy was also smart, sexy and had promised Helen the world. He was a lion, and I was a mangy lamb.

The play they were rehearsing was titled *Journey to Santa Fe*, written by Jeremy supposedly as a workshop vehicle for Helen. As he'd only known her for a couple of months, he must have written it fast. It was also his first full-length work, and it showed.

"I'm lost in my dreams," she said, sitting on a chair in the middle of the stage.

"No. You are lost on the road to Santa Fe," a young man intoned. I recognized him as the exchange student from Cambodia of whom the school was so proud. He was dressed now in an indeterminate animal suit, some sort of trickster spirit evidently, but looking more like a trained bear. At least they let him take the head off for rehearsals.

"Who are you?" Helen said, sobbing profusely, a modern Dorothy on the not-so-yellow brick road home.

She was so into her role she didn't even notice that I was there.

"I'm Rainbow Jackal and I've come to be your guide. Dry your tears, forget the tragedies of your past, the death of your mother, the incarceration of your father and come with me into a new world."

He held out his hairy paw. Helen hesitated for a few moments, her best acting so far. She looked toward stage right, stage left, at me, at Jeremy and eventually at the jackal who was now panting from the heat of his costume.

"I like the wheezing," Jeremy interrupted.

"Thanks," said the Jackal.

"I like the hesitation," I said to Helen. "You've got complete control of the audience."

"Quiet, all of you," she said. "You're wrecking my concentration."

After regrouping, she took the outstretched paw and stood.

"I will go with you, Jackal, but you must let me lead the way."

At those words the room began to spin like a surrealist film. It was as if she was speaking directly to me, warning me not to try to control this reanimation journey we were on together.

I got the message.

It was a terrible play but I was gratified to see that Helen actually could act. There she was, my formerly dead 75-year-old mom, pretending to be my sixteen-year-old disaffected cousin, playing the part of Deborah, Native American wanderer, hip-to-hip with a hairy Cambodian Jackal.

"How was I?" she said outside in the parking lot.

"Good," I said. "But the lines were rather weak. You'll be better as Lady Macbeth; let's leave it at that." *Macbeth* was the play Jeremy had planned for the fall.

Helen lit up a cigarette and blew some smoke in my face.

"Since when did you take up smoking again?" I said.

"Everybody in Drama Club smokes," she said. "I always enjoyed smoking back then. I figure I don't have to stop again until I'm forty."

Lately Helen had started referring to her first life as "back then," as if this was her real life and the other was just some history lesson from the ancient past.

"He's leaving his wife as soon as I graduate," she said. "He says he'll follow me to Yale. He means it. He weeps after we make love."

"He's an actor, Helen."

"What is it with you?"

She tossed her cigarette into the street and looked at me.

"This is who I am, like it or not, Elizabeth. I have a strong personality and a lot of charisma, unlike you."

She was right.

"You sure as hell can act," I said. "In spite of the crappy writing I found myself believing in you as Deborah, mystical road tripper searching the desert for the secrets to her soul." It was blatant manipulation, but I meant it, too, which I figured couldn't hurt our shaky connection.

"You did?" she said obviously delighted.

"We need to spend more time together," I said, taking advantage of the moment.

"I don't think so, Elizabeth," she said.

"Tomorrow is the fifth anniversary of your reanimation. We'll go shopping just for you and then I'll make you dinner with Raoul and David."

"And Jeremy," she said.

Helen didn't really care about celebrating her Reanimation Day except as an excuse to shop. Every year I kept hoping she'd thank me for bringing her back, for taking care of her, for anything, but it never happened. I think she believed it was me who should be grateful to her.

"And Jeremy," I said.

The next day after school I picked her up, and the two of us went into a dark, dank place that sold oriental antiques and smelled like anise and cinnamon.

Spending money was Helen's first love, of course, but today she actually had a shopping assignment from school. This spot, *Far East Antiques,* was on the top of the list.

"We're supposed to buy some object to represent a fictional character," she said.

"Why?" I said.

"How the hell should I know?" she said. "To try to get acquisitive people like me interested in literature, I guess. We're reading some book about women set in old China."

"You like to read," I said.

"I used to," she said, "when I was old and couldn't walk two steps without wetting myself. Now it's a different world. I don't need detective fiction to spice up my life. I have a million other things to do."

The proprietor approached us. She didn't look the part; she was blonde and sporty, not the wizened sage I was expecting.

"Are you looking for something special?" she asked us politely.

Helen was walking around picking things up and checking them out. This wasn't her kind of place but she was doing her best to enjoy it.

I wandered past the opium bottles and the Ming vases.

Helen returned to stand next to me.

"Do you have something for sale in the back?" I said to the owner. "Of museum quality or illegal, perhaps?"

"Elizabeth," she said nervously. "Let's get out of here. It's just a lot of old stuff."

The owner didn't miss a beat.

"How about a pair of shoes long ago worn by a woman with bound feet?"

"Perfect," I said. "Wrap them up."

They were tiny, dark blue things shaped like a comma and full of evil. After I paid her several hundred dollars, the owner put them in a wooden box with antique characters decorating the lid. As we left the shop, the owner swore us to secrecy about their origins.

"What will we do with them?" she whispered, evidently impressed that I'd bought her something so weird and so expensive. Shocking Helen was one of the main pleasures left to me in our relationship.

"I'm not sure," I said. "After 'show and tell' maybe dangle them from my rear view mirror."

She looked appalled.

"What do I say in class about the shoes?" she asked me.

"All women throughout history have had bound feet, meta-phorically speaking. Say that to your class. Tess, Hester…and make sure to tell everybody they're reproductions."

"I always did whatever I pleased," Helen mused. "Those weak Chinese women made their own damn choices."

"Well, never mind," I said. "You needn't pretend to be any-thing you aren't."

"I'm a Republican," she said by rote. "We hold people responsible for their own lives."

"Of course," I said. "Democrats just put people on the dole."

"What?"

"Forget it," I said.

"When I get my license I want an Astin Martin," she said as we got in the car.

For her Reanimation Celebration gift David and I had found a terrific counterfeiter to do Helen a birth certificate. It was going to be a surprise. Then she could get a real driver's permit.

"Why that car?" I said, delighted that we were actually having a conversation. "You seem more like the muscle car type, what with the Jaguar and all."

"Because that's what Hedda and I drove all over England," she said. "And it's a cute choice for a modern teen, don't you think?"

"Very cute," I said.

"I miss my mother," Helen said. "She looked exactly like a member of the British royal family."

After Mom's father died, before sending her off to boarding school, Hedda had taken them to England to get a better perspective, as she put it, from that lovely country of white people, castles and pudgy royals.

"You loved Hedda?" I said. "Didn't she drive your father to suicide?"

"Of course I loved her," she said. "What a silly question, Elizabeth. You can't help loving your own mother."

"I love you, Mom," I said.

She nodded.

"See what I mean?" she said.

"And I promise I'll never leave you like your dad did," I continued.

"It doesn't matter," she said. "You aren't him."

I was trying to look at my mom as a wounded bird but it still hurt my heart every time she spoke to me like that.

She could only be a wounded bird of prey.

"I hope Jeremy's waiting for me at home," she said.

"What about his wife? Is she back from filming?"

"He lies to her. What do you think? He's at rehearsal tonight."

I shrugged.

We were turning the corner onto our block. I hadn't spent this long with Helen in months, and, in spite of the usual bickering, it was feeling good. It was rekindling all that early hope I couldn't seem to let go of.

"There's Jeremy's car," she squealed.

It was parked in front of our house.

"You named me after the Queen of England, didn't you?" I said as we pulled into our driveway.

"What the hell are you talking about?" she said.

David came out to meet us carrying big fresh ginger cookies on a white plate.

"Happy birthday, Helen," he said holding the plate out to her. "I baked these for you."

She grabbed one and took a bite.

"Of course I didn't name you after the Queen," she said, still chewing.

"But there were other 'Elizabeths' before her," I kept on. It was strange I didn't even know about the origins of my own name.

Without answering me, she tossed her cookie back onto the plate and ran into the house to find her man.

"What are you talking about?" David asked, handing me a cookie of my own.

"Nothing," I said. "Just my name."

FOURTEEN

◆

"She seems to like Jeremy a lot," Raoul said later that evening. He took a sip from the wine they'd brought from the Aquarium cellar. We were sitting in the living room enjoying after dinner Reanimation Celebration drinks while Helen and Jeremy "rehearsed" in her room.

Suddenly he snapped his fingers as if he'd just remembered something.

"What?" I said.

"You're missing Helen," he said. "That's the trouble. She's spending all her free time with the drama coach."

"Who says I'm having trouble? I'm happy, happy, happy."

"You seem slightly faded, like a gray ghost of yourself," Raoul said. "You need a new passion. Maybe a dog or a girlfriend."

"Elizabeth is not you," David said to him impatiently.

"I don't do girlfriends any more," I said. "And Mom would probably kill the dog."

"I know what we can do with you," Raoul said. "You can come work for Stillwaters."

"You think working with a bunch of corpses is going to bring me back to life?"

I was pinching my cheeks to reawaken my evidently sagging energy when perky Helen and Jeremy came back into the room.

I lit the candles on her cake.

"Aren't you going to sing?" she said.

"Happy Reanimation Day," David and Raoul sang to her, "to you."

Jeremy and I joined in. Helen beamed, a queen with her subjects.

"How old are you really?" Raoul asked her as she cut the cake. I'd spent a lot of time making sure it was perfect, going over and over the spelling of 'reanimation' with the illiterate pastry clerk.

She stood up, glaring at him with pure hate.

"It's too complicated," David said, stepping into the breach.

"I've always liked older women," Jeremy said, pulling her back down. "And I've brought you a present." He pulled a box out of his pocket. "Open it up."

It was an antique ring with an amethyst set in gold.

"It's lovely," she said. He slipped it on her finger, a mock engagement ring.

"It was my grandmother's," he said.

I didn't believe him for a minute, but Helen did, and that was all that mattered.

"Oh Jeremy," she said and put her arms around his neck. "My mother used to have one like this too."

Then David and I gave Helen her forged birth certificate, rolled up and tied with a red velvet bow.

"So you can get a driver's license," I said.

"Where's my new car to go with it?" she said, glancing around. "Are the keys hidden someplace in the room? How fun."

"Later," I said. "After you pass the driver's test."

She pouted adorably and picked up something like a shoebox, immediately ripping off the ribbon. There was a card underneath that she didn't see.

"It's from me," Raoul said. "To keep you safe."

She opened the lid and gasped. It was a small pink handgun wrapped in red tissue paper.

"It's not loaded," Raoul went on. "But I figure just flashing it at a bad guy should do the trick."

She didn't know what to say. It was a lovely object, rosy mother of pearl with gold trim. It must have cost him a lot.

David snorted and Jeremy looked kind of freaked.

I'm not sure how good an idea it was to provide Helen with a gun, even if it was unloaded. Wouldn't it give her ideas? Was it in working order or just a pretty toy? And if it worked, how easy was it to buy ammo?

I looked at Raoul and shook my head.

"Maybe we'll keep it for her twenty-first celebration," I said.

"No way," Mom said, and grabbed the box.

He handed Helen the card. She opened it, giggled and then passed it around. On the cover was an old woman staring at a kid on a skateboard wearing a t-shirt that read, "Flash Me".

Inside the old lady was lifting up her shirt to reveal the bottoms of her desperately sagging breasts.

"You're only as old as you feel," the card read.

I threw it on the table.

A half an hour later, after opening a few more gifts, Helen yawned.

For some reason, Raoul still wasn't done needling her and Jeremy.

"Jeremy," he said. "Why don't we invite your wife to our next gathering?"

Helen grimaced. That woke her up.

"Elizabeth," she said. "Tell Raoul to shut up. Why is he picking on me?"

"You ask him," I said. "I dunno. Maybe he's drunk."

I figured Raoul was jealous of Helen. How could he help it? She was young, beautiful and had a boyfriend who evidently adored her.

"Don't you dare mention my wife again," Jeremy said, manning up.

"Why are you being so mean?" she said. "What has Jeremy ever done to you?"

"We all like Jeremy," Raoul said. "We just don't want you to be hurt."

Jeremy took a big gulp of expensive Bordeaux.

"I will not hurt Helen," he said. "I can assure you of that. Besides, if all goes well, Marilyn will be out of town for several months."

Jeremy's wife, Marilyn, we found out, had been a minor sitcom regular on *210 N. Rodeo Drive* and had just landed a part on the new reality show, *Lost in the Sewers of New York*.

"Your teeth are getting blue, Jer," Helen said irritably, "from the wine."

"You don't want her to come to dinner? Don't you love her?" I said, my face wide open with feigned innocence. The wine must have been making all of us mean.

"What is this?" Jeremy said. *"Who's Afraid of Virginia Woolf?"*

David patted him on the knee.

"I love her," Jeremy said. "I'm just not in love with her. We married too young. We're more like brother and sister." He rattled off all the dead marriage clichés in the book and even Helen rolled her eyes.

He got up and cleared the table, looking sick and tired of all of us.

"Jeremy and I are going back to rehearse in my bedroom," Helen said quietly after he left. "Do not interrupt us. We're performing *Breakfast at Tiffany's* next month at Bentwood. I'm the lead of course. Plus Jeremy said he had something to tell me. I'm guessing it's about leaving his wife."

"Wow," David said. "Congratulations."

She kissed him on the cheek.

"At least somebody's supportive."

She left without saying anything more, sashaying her hips like she owned the world. I had to hand it to her. Nothing got Helen down—suicide, death or the ravages of age. And even better than that, nothing made her doubt her own wonderfulness. What a gift.

"You're kidding," I said, with heat, to Raoul after she and Jeremy left the room. "You gave a crazy reanimated teenager a gun? Why didn't you ask me first? I'm her guardian, after all. And now it's a done deal."

"Listen to me. It's unloaded," he said. "Think of it as a pretty little keepsake."

"Are you trying to stir things up? Are you jealous that she's young? That she has a cute boyfriend?"

The two men were shocked at my audacity.

"Raoul," David said finally, "that gift did show a significant lack of judgment. You're doing much better now, but we'll have to look at this as a step backwards."

At that moment, as if to confirm David's remark, we heard two shots from Helen's bedroom. We all looked at each other, none of us wanting to move.

If we didn't move, it wasn't real.

"So it's loaded with blanks?" David said hopefully.

And then we heard three more. "I guess that wasn't television or a CD," Raoul said, "so it must have been blanks in the gun."

"Which one of us is going in there to discover the body?" David said jovially. "She's your mother. I'm tired from lifting all those dead people at work."

Nobody but me seemed to even entertain the thought that the shots were real. I put my head in my hands. I knew what those sounds were. They were the end of my life.

"Does anybody actually shoot anybody in *Breakfast at Tiffany's*?" Raoul said.

"Isn't anybody going to rush in here to see what happened?" Helen called from her doorway. "I just shot a real gun."

"OK, me," I said finally, standing up.

I stepped into her pretty white and blue bedroom, and the first thing I thought was how interesting a design all the red splatter made against the white bedspread.

Helen didn't look up. She was busy spraying Lysol Swiss Mountain Meadow air freshener all around Jeremy's body. He was lying on the bed, face up, eyes open wide.

"He's playacting," I said. "Jeremy, not nice."

"I only shot him a couple of times," she said. "The rest of the bullets are in the wall. At first I thought it wasn't loaded and then when it was I couldn't seem to stop shooting. You'll have to pry them out and then fill in the holes. Sorry about that. I've never used a gun before."

She leaned over the body and poked Jeremy's chest with her finger.

The blood, the smell. It hit me how real this was.

"Helen," I said slowly, "this is bad." I grabbed her arm to steady myself. I was almost falling over with the shock of it.

"I believe he just breathed his last. You're free to take him now," she said.

"We are not a body removal service," David said from the doorway. "God, what a couple of idiots you and Raoul are."

On cue, Raoul stepped into the room and began to shake like a scared dog.

"I'm so sorry," he whimpered.

"Why the hell didn't you at least check the gun?" I said.

"The guy who sold it to me, this old queen who cuts my hair, told me he hadn't used it in thirty years. I thought he meant he'd taken the bullets out."

David grabbed both of them, Raoul and Helen, by the collar, and shook them as hard as he could.

"I guess we can't make it look like suicide," Helen said, squirming out of David's grasp. "Not with all those bullets in his chest."

"Aren't you at all upset?" I shouted. "Can't you even fake a little emotion?"

Right now, I didn't care what happened to Helen. I was sick of her and disgusted. This was a hundred times worse than Pablo and the turtle and the snake. This confirmed all the evil I'd denied. She'd just kept on shooting.

"Just tell me why," I said, sitting down next to the corpse and beginning to weep. "I thought you loved him."

"He betrayed me." She leaned over him and began to smooth his hair away from his forehead. "He deserved it."

"Stop touching him like he's alive," I said, pushing her hand away.

"He told me that the stress of cheating on his stupid wife was giving him migraines. And then, the coup de gras." She paused, enjoying the self-justifications the way only a narcissistic reanimated sociopath could.

"What?" David said. "Just out of morbid curiosity, what did the poor schmuck tell you that he deserved to be killed?"

"That he was leaving me because Marilyn was pregnant, and he had to stay with her to raise their child. It was his duty as a man, particularly as the fetus had proved on ultrasound to be the male that he and his conniving wife decided they were going to name Jeremy junior."

"Oh, Helen," I said. And then all of a sudden I got this burst of raging energy that made me stand up and put my hands around her neck tight. "I could just kill you."

"Get her off me," she croaked.

Raoul pulled me off and tossed me back on the bed.

"Wouldn't you both have done the same thing?" she said, rubbing her neck. "I thought you'd be glad to be rid of him. He never brought over so much as a bottle of wine or a bit of Brie to share at dinner."

"He was a human being," I shouted again. "Maybe not a perfect specimen but no worse than most. It's not up to you who lives and dies."

We were all quiet after that. I looked at poor Jeremy, dead, and felt for him. He'd tried to love my mother the best way he knew how and look where it got him.

"Now what?" Helen said.

"It's all my fault," Raoul said. "Why did I give her that gun?"

"You are both going to jail for life," I said, firmly.

"I'll take the blame," Raoul said. "Here, wipe the gun clean and I'll put my fingerprints all over it."

"We can't call the police," David said, ignoring him. "Technically neither Raoul nor Helen even exists."

"I'm a child. I can't go to jail," she said. "Besides I wouldn't survive there. I'd be torn limb from limb by all the desperate lesbians. You know that. We all need to focus on the extenuating circumstances and hide the body."

"What extenuating circumstances?" I said. "You're a serial murderer, a sociopath. You started with animals like they all do. Torturing cats and pythons and crabs. You have to be stopped."

I picked up the phone. David grabbed my hand.

"Elizabeth," he said. "We're not calling the police. We're going to take the body to Stillwaters and get rid of it. Raoul and Helen will take care of the rest of the evidence."

With that all the air went out of me and I sort of deflated. I didn't really want to send my own mother to jail or strangle her myself. I just wanted all this part to be over.

"Go get a sheet," Helen said. "We'll roll him up in that first. But nothing over 300 count."

We put the sheet on the floor, pushed Jeremy off the bed onto it and wrapped him up so we could drag him out the door.

"He's fucking heavy," David said, pulling one end towards the door. Luckily it was dark out so nobody would see us, especially the Garcias.

We drove in silence for most of the way to Stillwaters and I thought about what a fiasco this whole Mom reanimation thing had been. Even Raoul, the sex-addict, hadn't actually hurt anything except maybe David's heart.

"Don't you think there's something we still need to figure out about age manipulation loosening impulse control?" I asked as we passed the fire station.

"I told you Raoul's much better than he was," David said quickly. "He finally seems to have gotten most of his libido under control."

"He gave my mother a loaded gun."

That shut him up.

We drove David's SUV into the back of Stillwaters.

I'd just attempted to strangle my own mother. I was pulling a dead body out of the car. If she'd murdered her boyfriend because he'd hurt her feelings, she could do the same to me, to anybody.

We carried Jeremy inside to the operating room and I started to help David undress him.

He pointed to a huge vat.

"It's full of noxious chemicals for the bodies of the people who only want to freeze their heads," he explained. "We'll toss him in there."

"OK," I said, pulling off Jeremy's socks.

"He didn't have a clue, poor schmuck," he said. "I wonder what he saw in Helen."

"Pretty skin, good brains, a quirky take on life," I said. "She's always been very popular, in both lives, amazingly enough. Some people adore narcissists."

"He's heavier than he looked," David said, working a complicated hoist to get the body into the tank.

"This is so nice of you," I said, stirring the hot brew like a big instant pudding.

"The system is manufactured in Sweden," he said. There were four spigots a couple feet from the ground for the liquid drainage labeled FAT, BILE, BLOOD and OTHER.

"Helen would never do this for me," I said.

"She'd never have to. You would never shoot your girlfriend."

"You're right," I said and because of that comment, Minerva's pretty face popped into my mind, the one person in the world who said she really loved me.

"He was fattier than he appeared," David said.

"Why separate the liquids?"

"Easier disposal. Less environmental impact."

He seemed to have very few qualms about being an accessory to the crime. Maybe after doing so many reanimations actual mortality was less real for him than the rest of us.

When we were done, we sat down in David's office, side by side on the couch.

"What now?" I said. I was shaking and sweating. Things were too real.

"Tomorrow Helen and Raoul will patch the bullet holes in her room and get rid of the gun. Did anybody know she and Jeremy were lovers?"

"Kendra maybe."

"Well, have Helen get her story straight if the police happen to come around."

"No problem," I said. "She's an actress."

David handed me a Scotch. Then he put his arm around my shoulders.

"Two lonely old homos with a tumbler of Scotch," he said.

I didn't exactly love his arm around me but I didn't hate it either.

"You're not so lonely," I said, squirming a little bit.

"You're safe now," he said, holding tighter. "No body, no murder."

"You saved my life," I said.

"I know," David said and then he kissed me on the ear.

I shivered. Another sip of the Scotch and I was dizzy.

"I mean you've got Raoul, of course," I said. "You aren't really lonely."

Was David actually coming on to me? How creepy.

"I think it's highly unlikely your mother will kill anybody again," David continued. He took my hand in his big warm paw.

"That's good."

He said something else but I wasn't listening. I was thinking about how I wished I were sitting with somebody else. Maybe Minerva.

By now David was totally settled in against my body.

"David," I said. "Don't get too comfortable."

I pulled my hand away.

"I know, I know," he said, straightening up. We both finished our drinks.

We sat on the couch a few minutes longer in silence. I pictured Jeremy's body melting in the vat, his hands, his eyes, his legs. I didn't want to cry anymore, especially not with David in his cuddly mood, so instead, I thought about Helen.

"I'd like to cut her hands off with an ax," I said.

The hot anger sort of cooled the awful Jeremy thoughts.

David whistled.

"She'd have these little stubs," I continued. "She couldn't paint her goddamn fingernails; she couldn't shoot a gun or wield a knife."

"Jesus Christ," he said.

"Don't be so shocked," I said. "You who manipulated Raoul's age upwards without asking him. You who played God."

"Why don't you cut off her feet while you're at it?" David said. "Then you could have complete control. You'd have to give her baths and roll her from place to place."

Honestly, for a moment the idea appealed to me. How else was I ever going to manage her?

I smiled wickedly. She deserved it. She'd killed a perfectly decent human being just because she could.

"You go on home alone," David said then. "I don't think I can stomach the blood splatter etcetera another time. I know that sounds funny with the kind of work I do but I've never actually been around murder before."

I walked out into the dark, found my car and got in. Then I began to hit the steering wheel with my forehead. I wasn't drunk anymore but I was as miserable as I'd ever been in my life. I was about to implode.

Almost on remote control, I drove over to Minerva's house and rang the bell. After a moment, the little eye in the middle of the front door blinked open and Min let me in. She was wearing a white cotton bathrobe with her black hair pulled back in a ponytail. I was l a person without a home.

"Come in, come in," she said, as if she wasn't surprised to see me.

"I can't tell you what's happened," I said, sinking into her big couch.

She handed me a glass of water.

"You look so tired," she said, smoothing my hair out of my eyes. "It's Helen I bet."

"Yes," I said. "I should go back."

"Why don't you stay here a little while? I can leave you alone if you need a place to think."

"No," I said. "Sit down next to me. Hold me in your arms, tight."

She did. She wrapped a blanket around us and held on to me as if we were in a tiny boat on a rough sea. Somehow I knew I was finally safe.

"Is everybody asleep?" I asked her, nuzzling my face in her neck.

"Yes," she whispered. "Kendra and her dad are both heavy sleepers."

I kissed her on the mouth.

Minerva smelled so good and she was so warm. I remembered being in bed with her all those years ago but it had never felt like this. I kissed her again and then we lay down on the wide couch and made love.

I let her kiss me all over my body. I put my mouth on her breasts. I moaned and climbed inside her like I never had before.

We lay together for a little while afterwards and I could feel all the fear and anger and need drain out of me. At least for now.

"You are so much softer than before," Min said into my ear.

That's when I knew I had to leave.

When I got back home, Raoul and Helen were waiting for me at the breakfast table. Helen had pinned her hair up and was wearing a one-piece bathing suit, the slick kind you swim laps in. Raoul was drinking a cup of coffee in his boxer shorts. The washing machine was running and there was a big pile of bloody linen in the center of the kitchen floor.

Helen pointed at the stuff.

"You'll have to get rid of all that. It's got his DNA all over it."

"We undressed so we could rinse off all the blood," Raoul said. It was hard work what we did. It was disgusting."

"Explain to me again why you gave her a gun?" I said.

"Leave him alone," Helen said. "I promise not to do it again. I've learned my lesson. We both agreed that our inhibitions and judgment aren't what they used to be before we got reanimated."

"Amazing," I said. "Some real insight."

"I'm just saying," she continued. "You reanimated us. It's David's technique. I never was tempted to shoot anybody in my first life."

"You're blaming me and David?"

"No more guns," Raoul said. "It's in that pile of evidence."

"We'll melt it all down in the vat tomorrow," I said.

"No more animals in the house either," I said just in case Helen was already thinking about how to slake those uninhibited killer appetites.

"No?"

"No," I said. "Except maybe a goldfish. The kind that swim around in circles all day long."

"The kind you can flush down the toilet when they die," she said.

FIFTEEN

◆

Although the neighbors must have heard the shots, the police never even came to talk to us. What luck! Hard to believe, but evidently Helen had kept her affair with Jeremy secret enough that there were no suspicions. Even from Kendra, who was still her friend, although Kendra had turned out to be too smart and ambitious to have much in common with Helen. The occasional shopping binge was all that seemed to hold them together, and I'm pretty sure Helen paid for everything they bought.

Suddenly Minerva and Kendra's dad separated. Min told me on the phone that she'd decided to be a lesbian again and had started dating somebody she met at a beach bar for dykes and their friends called Sweet Sailing, a place we used to like. Min promised Kendra that they'd always be related, which seemed to me a strangely vague way to reassure your ex-step daughter that you weren't abandoning her.

I felt sorry for Kendra, who was clearly deeply bonded with her stepmother, the only mother she'd really known.

So once a month I began to invite the two of them to dinner just in case Kendra hadn't seen Min. Sometimes after the meal, while the girls hung out in Helen's newly redecorated bedroom, Min liked to have an extra glass of wine and complain about me.

"We should be together," she'd say. "We love each other."

"No we don't," I'd say. "I was scared and lonely that night at your house. You already have a new girlfriend."

"Only because you won't have me," she said. "What the hell is wrong with you?"

"Relationships are about give and take," I said.

"I have no idea what you're talking about," Min said. "You don't either. You're just saying gibberish to put me off."

"You always think a relationship is supposed to fill you up," I said. I was sounding like some self-help book but I couldn't stop.

"Like you're one to talk about relationships," she said. "You like sex and a warm body next to you in bed. That's it."

She was probably right.

"Well, so?" I said. "Are you spending enough time with Kendra?"

"Of course," Min said. "It's none of your business anyway."

"What is it you want from me?" I said. I grabbed one of Helen's cigarettes off the table and lit it.

"We all know about Helen."

"What?" I said and coughed.

"We know that she's your foster daughter that you got to take my place because you need so much control."

I laughed and put the cigarette out. So that was the story going around town.

"Helen told you that or did you and Kendra come up with it on your own?"

"It's obvious really. It's all because of your mother who made you feel worthless. You can't risk letting an adult close."

"Fine," I said. "I guess somebody's started therapy again."

Minerva didn't know anything important about me and never had. In that sense she was a lot like Mom.

Helen dealt with the uproar at school about the missing Jeremy by pretending to believe he was still alive. She even had buttons made up with his picture on them reading: "Where am I?" and the phone number of the local cops. She kept her amnesia and abduction theory going by quoting details from old cases she'd looked up on the Internet.

She got an A on her abduction research essay for social studies, and it wasn't a sympathy grade either. The paper she wrote was passionate and creative, charting original statistics about lost male high school teachers in their thirties.

Helen read it aloud at a special memorial assembly and dedicated it to Jeremy, which I thought was laying it on a bit thick, but that was Helen for you. She knew how to work a crowd. Marilyn, his now obviously pregnant wife, even kissed her on the cheek when it was over.

I sat in the back of the auditorium watching everything and trying not to look guilty.

How do you look innocent?

"Hi there, Elizabeth," a voice called out from across the aisle. I jumped. It was the principal, Jim Gibson, looking better than he ever had before. He was wearing nice khakis and a blue shirt. He had cool glasses too. The frames were those black circles that self-conscious architects wear, except that his looked just right on his small face. Natural.

I met him halfway and put out my hand.

"Hi there," I said, "Mr. Gibson."

"Jim," he said. "Helen is putting on quite a show in honor of poor Jeremy. He always said she had a gift."

I remembered that Jim had a sense of humor but I decided not to risk joking back, in view of the sad occasion and all.

"Is there anything I can do?" I said. "I know how much Jeremy meant to her and to the school both."

"Like bake cookies?" he said.

"Well," I smiled, stalling. I still couldn't read his tone. Sardonic, flirtatious, hungry?

"Actually, we do need somebody who can teach a little bit of American Lit. Marilyn, Jeremy's wife, has agreed to cover his drama classes."

"Really?" I said. "She's an amazing woman to step in at a time like this. What happened to the gig in New York?"

Woops. How did I know about that?

"She didn't mention it," Jim said. "I guess she lost heart."

What a nice man Jim Gibson was. What empathy. For the first time I felt really bad for Marilyn. Really, really bad.

And guilty as hell for having brought Mom back from the dead to do the deed.

"My last profession was owning a house-cleaning establishment," I said, giving him my verbal resume.

"Perfect," Jim said. "You're hired. Just as a substitute for a few weeks, until we can get somebody who knows what they're doing."

Which is how I started teaching a group of very smart Bentwood sophomores Alice Walker's *The Color Purple*. Blessedly my mother wasn't in the class.

But Kendra was.

Helen was pissed when she heard I was going to spend a couple hours a day at her school, mostly with her best friend.

She didn't say it in so many words but by now I could read her like a book.

Her cheeks got bright red and her mouth went tight over her perfect teeth.

"So how are you going to dress on the first day?" she asked. I should have known that would be the big question. The surface was all Helen could see.

"I haven't thought about it." I paused. "Did you tell Kendra you were my adopted daughter?"

"Of course not," she said. "Why would I do that?"

"I don't know," I said. "That's what she and Min think." I didn't tell her the rest of the speculation, that she was a substitute for my bad mother. I didn't tell her that because that part was the truth.

"Just don't wear anything too dowdy or too sexy," she said. "No extremes. I don't want you to embarrass me."

"All I have is dowdy," I said. "But I'll keep it simple. I'll be practically invisible. Shirt, pants, sweater."

"And not too gay," she said, slamming her bedroom door behind her.

I went into our beautiful living room and sat staring at the ocean with a copy of Walker's novel in my hands. I was pretty excited to have a real job for a little while and to be with some kids who weren't Helen.

And lots better than Raoul's idea of hanging out with the corpses at Stillwaters.

I'd have to be careful with Marilyn though. I was an accessory to the murder of her husband after all. Who knew how well I would handle a face to face with a fresh and pregnant widow?

I dove into my preparation.

The next morning, after reading *The Color Purple* twice, highlighting entire paragraphs and taking notes on all sorts of critical essays about race, love, men, women and just about every other human issue there was, I drove to work. Helen sat beside me in the car, staring out the window.

It reminded me of our first drive after she got reanimated. New beginnings and all that. But this time I wasn't quite as optimistic.

"Look," she said as we turned into the Bentwood faculty parking lot.

"What?"

"There's a boy and girl having sex in the bushes. How disgusting is that? At eight in the morning."

"Where?"

"Do something," she said to me. "You're a teacher."

"What?"

"Get a room," Mom shouted at the giant lavender hydrangea next to the entrance. "I'll pay you ten bucks if you stop the car and give the Bentwood girl a demerit," she said to me. "She's such a whore."

I saw that she was right. A guy and girl were busily putting their uniforms back on. The boy was evidently from the brother school down the street.

"Whore!!!" she shouted.

"Does this happen often?" I asked her. "I mean this is an elite prep school."

"You're asking if rich kids fuck?"

"Don't talk like that, Helen. You know better. What I mean is can't they afford to get a room?"

I parked the car in the faculty lot and watched her jump out. Instead of giving me some teacher tips or showing me to my classroom, she couldn't wait to get away from me. Why would I be surprised?

When I found my classroom, everybody was there, waiting to get a good look at me, Helen's cousin/adoptive mom.

About twenty girls dressed in uniform white shirts and blue skirts, were staring at me, each desperately trying to make herself an individual with dangly earrings or hair ribbons made of a man's tie.

I was pretty disappointing, I think. I was wearing my one and only dress, a black wool number with a matching jacket that I usually only put on for funerals and fund-raisers.

I'd have to win them over with my charming personality.

I looked around and noticed that, luckily, the school had removed all of Jeremy's personal effects. What was left were literary posters about terms like metonymy and people like Kafka, looking distinctly beetle-ish himself.

"Hey, Elizabeth," Kendra said. "Just promise you won't make me the black poster child for this novel."

"Don't worry," I said. "I know all about teacher/student boundaries."

I'd done well in school, often falling in love with the good women teachers. Theirs were the classes I excelled in, writing essays and lab reports with all the passion I could muster.

"Excellent insights," they'd write in spidery black ink. I'd savor any positive comment as if it were part of a love letter yet to be sent.

I wondered if any of these girls would get crushes on me. Or would I be too plodding and self-conscious to inspire the dreamy stuff I'd felt?

The extraordinary thing was that I didn't need to worry at all. I turned out to be a terrific teacher, if I do say so myself.

Who knew I'd have rapport with teenage girls and exude a love of literature on top of that?

Now that I thought back on it, those teachers had probably saved my life.

Immediately, I was encouraged. Maybe because I was new, or a woman, or Kendra's friend, right from the beginning they answered every question I asked.

"Why does the author have Celie use dialect?"

Answer: "Because she's poor and simple, and that's the way African Americans talked."

"Why does she write to God?"

Answer: "God's all she had until Shug."

"What's her relationship with Shug?"

Answer: "They were lovers."

This answer was supposed to be 'friends' but honestly, what could I do about it? They were lovers. Shug taught Celie how to feel between her legs and in her heart.

"Were they lesbians?" Kendra asked after class.

"Shug was like a mother to her," I said. "Like Minerva and you."

At that moment, Helen popped in with a greasy plate of cafeteria hash browns for me. She'd taken to coming to visit me frequently, to demonstrate ownership, no doubt.

"You aren't supposed to be in here alone with a student, Elizabeth."

"Oh for heaven's sake, Helen. Kendra is our friend."

"As a lesbian you should be extra careful about appearances. Leave your door open at least."

"Oh Helen," Kendra said. "Be nice."

She tossed the hash browns on my desk, a mound of ketchup sliding onto the front of *The Color Purple*. Then she walked out, leaving the door open wide.

Kendra stood up to leave.

"She's jealous, Elizabeth. Don't worry about it. I'll buy her lunch. It's chile relleno casserole, her favorite."

There were still a few things about Helen I didn't know.

"I won't be here much longer anyway. I'm just a sub."

"By the way, did Min tell you she was getting back together with Dad?"

"Is that good news?" For some reason my heart kind of sank. I brushed it off as low blood sugar. I took a bite of the potatoes Helen had brought.

"Of course," Kendra said. "She's a lot of fun to be around. But, you know, I can totally see you two together too."

Sometimes I wished I could be more like Min, flitting from lover to lover, gender to gender, like a hummingbird, tasting a bit here and there. Sometimes I wished I could be anybody besides me.

SIXTEEN

♦

The kids on campus knew me enough by now to wave or shout "hi" when I walked near their groups. If I'd had the right degrees and needed the money, I would have called Bentwood my career in a second. Especially after Helen graduated. As for now, she kept lurking around in corners as if she wanted to catch me doing something wrong. I couldn't imagine what she thought it would be.

I took the remaining hash browns to the faculty lounge to reheat in the microwave, which is where poor pregnant Marilyn was eating cereal and drinking milk for two. When I saw her, alone at the table nearest the door, I quickly turned to go back out.

"Hey," she said. "You're Helen's cousin. You're the one taking Jeremy's honors American Lit. Come here and sit down."

I carried my icky little paper plate over to her table and put it next to her sliced fruit and oatmeal.

"Yuck," she said, looking at my stuff. "That's what they sell here? No wonder Jeremy was getting a pot."

"Sorry," I said and tossed it out.

"Too late," she said and just barely made it to the sink to throw up.

"Morning sickness?" I asked when she came back.

She wiped her mouth. Marilyn was movie star pretty even when she puked. She'd pulled back her brown hair so it didn't get in the way when she was sick.

"Maybe," she said. "I also do it sometimes when I realize Jeremy's really dead."

She wiped her mouth with a paper towel.

"You don't have hope he'll be found?"

"No. In fact, I'm sorry to say I always knew this would happen."

A few other teachers were sitting at the big table across the room but they weren't listening. Evidently they hadn't even noticed when Marilyn threw up. One old guy was reading the paper and two women younger than me were giggling about a television show they'd seen. Somebody had written 'clean up your own crap' on the white board behind them.

"Like a premonition?"

It was so strange to be pretending I was somebody else: a nice, normal person who was honestly concerned about a probably widowed colleague. It was surprisingly easy. Since Mom returned as a kid, I'd had a lot of practice pretending.

I poured myself a cup of coffee.

"Does the puke smell?" Marilyn said, cupping her breath.

"No," I said, sitting back down. It didn't. She didn't. She was the type of lovely woman who didn't ever smell. I wondered why she'd married such a creep.

"Well," she said, getting back into the subject of Jeremy. "It wasn't like a premonition exactly. More like he was too good for this world. More like he was an angel on earth for just a little while. To give me Jeremy junior."

I couldn't help it. I choked.

"Is your coffee too hot?" she asked.

The bell rang for the end of lunch but neither of us had classes, so we didn't move. The other faculty members rushed out, tossing their paper cups into the recycling bin on the way.

I looked at Marilyn with sudden and withering disdain. She and her angel deserved each other.

How could such a dumb woman be an actress, even a bit player in a reality show? It made me understand how Jeremy would have a thing with Mom.

"It's good to think of him that way," I said with condescension. "As a heavenly presence. I'm sure it helps."

"I actually think he was having an affair with a student," Marilyn said flatly, as if she was a different person all of a sudden. It was scary. It was almost like Helen.

"No," I said. I put my hands on my lap so she wouldn't see how badly they had begun to shake.

Now, I knew she was a great actress. She could get me to believe anything she wanted to, even the truth.

"Jeremy was having an affair and I was too. But he didn't know about mine. Men are stupid. They think they're the only people in the world."

Whose baby was she carrying? Had Helen killed Jeremy for nothing?

"Marilyn," I said. "Why are you telling me this? You don't even know me."

She looked at me for a while and then I understood. She thought Helen was the other woman.

"It doesn't matter now," she said, eating some more of her oatmeal. "I gave him an ultimatum, the clichéd 'her or me,' but evidently that was too much for him to handle. He couldn't bring himself to make the decision. Men are such babies."

"So you think he killed himself?"

I put my hand on hers.

"Of course," she said. "He'd always been the artistic moody type. That's why I fell in love with him. But that kind of love doesn't last long."

I didn't ask her where she thought his body was or how he did it, although I was wondering about her lack of interest in the details. I mean, weren't most suicides discovered right away?

But all the same this woman was wise. Maybe in denial a little bit, but wise about men. Wimps like Jeremy must get real boring after a few years. Helen probably would have lost interest herself if he'd given her time.

"Maybe it was a good thing he killed himself," Marilyn went on now, cold as ice. "Seeing the infant would have broken his heart. If you know the show, my lover was Gregory from the *Sewers of New York*."

I'd seen the cast recently in a newspaper photo, taken right before the end of the season. Gregory was a burly Asian guy with Maori tattoos. Nothing close to Jeremy's gene pool there.

In the picture, Marilyn was standing next to him looking skinny and oily and buff. The baby didn't show.

"Why did you call Jeremy an angel and all of that?"

"It's what I've been telling everyone. That's what they want to hear. When you choked, I figured I could trust you."

"So why didn't you just leave him if you disliked him so much?" I asked, thinking how much easier that decision would have made my life and Helen's.

"I'm an old-fashioned woman, in some ways," she said, surprisingly. "For better or for worse actually means something to me."

Marilyn believed what happened was that her husband couldn't bring himself to choose between herself and Helen. Of course I didn't tell her the truth, that what he'd actually done was to choose Marilyn and Jeremy Junior when bang, Helen shot him dead.

"Well, gotta go get prepared for rehearsal," she said. She covered up her belly with a white linen jacket and picked up her bowl.

"I'll do that," I said.

"Oh, no sweat," she said, and went to soap up the sink where she'd been sick.

How easy she made everything seem. Affairs, pregnancy, loss of a spouse, beginning of a new life.

"What's the next play going to be?" I asked.

"*Arsenic and Old Lace*," she said without blinking an eye. "Your Helen is the lead. Of course I don't need to tell you what a natural gift she has."

"I'm so sorry," I said, before I could stop myself.

"Don't worry about a thing," she answered as if she understood exactly what I was trying to say.

SEVENTEEN

◆

That evening I knocked on Helen's bathroom door while she was taking a bath.

"What?" she said. I could smell her expensive bath powders through the door, eucalyptus and lavender.

"Can I come in and talk?" I said.

"You're still mad at me," she called through the door. Then the sound of her favorite soft jazz station being turned up.

"Why would I be mad at you?" Needless to say, the only way I could enjoy Helen now was to live in the present moment. What I felt about her was so far beyond the word *mad* I almost couldn't bear to think about it.

"That I shot Jeremy. You spent lunch break with that Marilyn and you liked her. On top of that I think I flunked Algebra II. What can I do about it? I'm bad to the bone."

"Helen, you should be playing with your friends at school instead of watching me so much. Don't worry. I love you. Everything's fine."

It wasn't fine. I could easily have strangled her several times a day. I was sometimes sick with shame. And yet when I opened the door, she took my breath away. She was sitting up in the tub, surrounded by candles, her body in the golden light more beautiful than I'd ever seen it before. In fact, I hadn't seen her completely undressed in years and, of course, never at this age. Not that she was modest. In fact, she'd always believed in her body as a gift to the rest of us, even when she was old, sagging and scabby.

In those days Doreen and I were to consider ourselves lucky to apply cream to her gnarly feet and dress her bruises and wounds.

I didn't want to see Helen naked. Maybe I thought I'd experience something unpleasant inside myself, an awkward attraction, an unnatural response, given the mixed- up nature of our ages and relationship. Or maybe I couldn't stand to see her so vulnerable. Whatever it was I looked away.

"You should look at me," she said. "It doesn't get any better than this."

I made myself look at her clearly. Her breasts were full and her stomach was flat. Her arms and legs were tanned and tapered. Her brown hair was pulled off her neck in a big gold barrette. I could see that she'd been crying; her eyes were red, but not like she'd gotten soap in them.

"You do have a great body, Helen," I said.

"Want to wash my back?"

She handed me a washcloth and bent forward.

"I haven't been crying," she said.

Lightly I washed and rinsed her skin. The musky scent of the soap and the warmth of the water sent me into a dream. Being with Mom was just as dangerous as it had ever been. She was so soft and alive I could hardly stand it. I could hardly bear how much I still loved her and wanted her to love me.

"Ah, Helen," I said. I squeezed the warm water from the sponge over her neck. I had the strange thought that I was baptizing her, cleansing her rotten soul.

"What?" she said. "I'm listening. Sometimes you take so long to say what you mean."

"I understand why you shot him. You couldn't help it."

"Exactly, that's what I've been saying. I couldn't help it." She sighed deeply and bent her head towards the bathwater.

Slowly, I rubbed my hand around on her back. It was a deeply tender touch I'd never allowed myself before.

"I love you so much,' I said and because she couldn't see me, I began to cry.

"That feels wonderful," she said. "I love you too."

There it was, the thing I'd been waiting all my life to hear. The big breakthrough moment the therapist had told me about.

I rinsed her neck and then I kissed it. I don't know what I was expecting to happen, fireworks maybe or Jesus crashing through the ceiling on a fluffy cloud.

I left the bathroom before she got out of the tub and went to lie down in my bedroom. I opened the window and smelled the ocean breezes on my face.

All I could think was that I'd sold my soul to stay close to my murdering Helen when I knew in my heart she'd only get worse.

After dinner, we sat on the couch in our nightgowns and tuned to a repeat of Sewers *of New York.* I closed the curtains and turned off the lights, the way Helen liked to watch TV, so that there were no distractions.

"You really want to watch Marilyn?" I said. It was playing on our huge flat screen TV that she'd insisted we put right over the fireplace as if it was a work of art.

"You think she's attractive?" she asked me when Marilyn came on, every pore shimmering in high def.

"Kind of predictable looking," I said. "Even features, small nose, actress-y."

"I really loved him, you know," Helen said. "It was stupid that he was married but how could I help that? You love the one you love. She got pregnant just to tie him to her tighter. It's a classic desperation move."

"I know," I said.

I didn't think Mom could actually love someone in the usual sense of the word, where things like empathy, self-sacrifice and respect usually played out, but I tried to hear her out.

"Jeremy was better than the boyfriend I lost when my father died, although, in a way, both boyfriends left me."

"What a piece of work you are," I said. "You're the only person in the world who could kill a perfectly innocent person in cold blood and call it self-defense."

"You should try it," she said.

And with that, I flashed unpleasantly on strangling her with the cord of her bathrobe.

Next, on the screen, Marilyn was slithering through some gunky sewage in a bikini with a miner's lamp attached to her head.

"That woman's husband is the whole reason I wanted to come back as a kid," Helen said, tiny silver tears dripping down her cheeks. They reminded me of jewelry you'd buy on a chain at Tiffany's.

I took her hand in mine. Half the time, talking to Helen left me so cold I could hardly sit still but tonight was different, probably because of the nice moment in the bathroom.

On the television, Marilyn was ravenously eating something from a bucket with her hands. It looked like gooey ocean seaweed, with polyps, tubular stalks and big brown leaves. A tolerance for the gross-out factor must have been a key part of the competition.

Funny how she'd thrown up at the mention of Jeremy's name in the lunchroom.

"If she hadn't gotten pregnant, Jeremy was going to leave her. He was going to take me to London to study acting, before Yale. Or after. I can't remember."

"Yes," I said.

"What the hell am I supposed to do now? I am so lonely, Elizabeth."

There was more crying but she didn't move her hand away from mine. I took that as a small victory.

"Marilyn says you're gifted. You can still go to acting school."

"Right now, I just want another boyfriend, one who won't leave me like everybody else."

On the TV Gregory was climbing over piles of slimy garbage to get to Marilyn, his secret favorite teammate.

"Help me," Marilyn was whispering, seductively.

"I won't leave you." I said to Helen.

"You mean that, Elizabeth?" she said, her eyes filling up.

We looked at each other for the longest time. It might have been a French film.

"I promise I won't leave you," I repeated, with great emotion.

Had all the effort with Mom's reanimation, the frustration, the sadness, the murder, the shame, had it suddenly all paid off?

"Well, of course you won't," she said, pulling her cold hand away from mine so she could reach for the remote.

Or had the whole evening, from bathtub to *Sewers* been acting?

Of course it had.

The truth was that my huge unending need for Mom was making me insane.

At that moment on *Sewers*, Gregory made it to Marilyn. He reached out his arms and pulled her through the slime towards him. She put her greasy head on his shoulder and whimpered like a small animal.

"Marilyn is such a fraud," Helen said and changed the station to a shopping channel, her favorite from before when she was old and lame.

"Well, so I guess I'll go to bed now," I said, lingering on the couch.

More than anything I wanted her to tell me to stay. I got up and stood in the doorway for a few seconds, watching her get comfortable, pulling a blanket up to her nose. She turned off the lamp.

On the screen some B movie star was energetically selling gold necklaces and seashell earrings, pandering to all the shopping addicts as if these things could save your life.

"You look so big standing there in the doorway with the light behind you," she giggled. "Like you're a fuzzy monster out of a children's book. Aren't you going to kiss me goodnight?"

"Kiss you?"

Maybe she'd mixed me up with Doreen.

"Yes," she said.

So I did it. Twice in one day. This time I kissed her on the forehead, something I hadn't done since right after she came back.

I shivered.

"What's wrong?" she said.

"Nothing. I just got a chill. Your forehead is like ice."

Then I handed her another blanket and went to bed.

I lay in bed for hours that night staring at the ceiling. Every one of my senses was acute. To the east, I could hear the cars on the coast highway taking the curves too fast; the other direction, I listened to the waves crashing and the sea lions calling to each other with quick joyous barks; my legs felt jittery in an unpleasant way. I was too hot and then I was too cold, so I kicked off the blankets and then pulled them back up.

I wanted to scream.

It was like something was trying to climb out of me. Something I didn't want to see.

I took a pill and then blessedly, I fell asleep.

The first part of my dream I can't remember, but at the end, Marilyn and I were in a king-sized bed, head to toe, both giving birth.

"This is so fun," she said as Jeremy Junior popped out from between her legs. I grabbed him and he peed in my face.

"Sorry," he said. "I just had to go wee wee. Nothing personal."

I held him up for his mother to see.

"You look just like Jeremy," she said, because in my dream it was true.

Then a gigantic wave rippled through my abdomen as I delivered my own baby in a wash of fluid.

I was so excited to see what I'd produced.

"Ick," Marilyn said. "What's all that? Where's the nurse? Somebody needs a wipe up."

"Where's my baby?" I shouted at her, lifting up my head to look.

"Here," she said, putting it on my stomach so I could see. The body was sharp and hot and wet.

At first I thought it was going to be an infant version of Mom.

But it wasn't. It was a monster with the head of a lizard and the body of shark. It flicked its tongue at me and whispered something indecipherable.

"What's it saying?" I called.

But Marilyn was too busy with Jeremy Junior to translate. He was already sucking on her breast and cooing with delight. My baby bit me on the stomach and then let out a throaty rasp.

"Meat," it said, this time clearly. Then I woke up. The first thing I did was reach down to see if I'd soiled myself; the dream seemed that real. But luckily I hadn't. I closed my eyes and thought about what I'd seen.

Mom had just called me a monster on my way out of the living room. That was the easiest explanation. I guess I was my own baby. A reptile from *The Sewers of New York.*

Then I remembered a dream book saying you shouldn't think too hard about symbolic meanings when you have a big dream, that the best thing to do is to let your intuitive self take charge.

What my intuitive self told me was the exact opposite of what most people would think. A monster coming out of your body means bad things, doesn't it?

But as I lay there on the dawn of the new day, I was suddenly consumed by the notion that the dream meant I should have a baby of my own. It might be a monster but at least it wouldn't be Mom.

Even Minerva agreed, in her own way. Hadn't she told me she thought Helen was my daughter, adopted to take the place of my cold mom? Hadn't she wanted us to have a baby when we were together?

I lay back down in bed and pulled the covers over my head.

All I needed was a man. To this end, I began to regret that I hadn't had sex with David the night we melted Jeremy down in the vat and got drunk. Not that I would have necessarily gotten pregnant. I wasn't so young anymore and who knew if I was still even ovulating.

David was smart and he did care about me, although as a friend, that might make things messy. Worse, his chin was, by anybody's measure, receding.

Barack Obama wasn't available.

I closed my eyes and Jim Gibson floated past. He could be a possibility. After all, he had hit on me that one time. He'd probably do anything I wanted, including making a baby and then staying the hell out of my life. He had a good chin, and, although he was on the smallish side, I had a feeling we'd make a good looking, smart kid.

"Anonymous" was probably safer than either of them but something about that didn't feel right, even if they gave you a check list of preferences when you bought the vial.

EIGHTEEN

◆

I fell back asleep and when I woke up again Helen was yanking on my covers.

"Hurry up," she said. "I can't be late to school. I already have four demerits this month."

I threw on my black wool dress and grabbed my briefcase. I loved my job except for having to get there so early in the morning.

"OK, we're here, just in time," I said as I turned into the parking lot at Bentwood.

"So I'll get a ride home from Marilyn," Helen said, grabbing her book bag.

Jim's secretary, a tall lanky gal named Sue, was stationed near the bushes to discourage any more early morning trysts.

"Hi Sue," I said, putting my window down. "Any action?"

"No, thank God," she said. "I guess I'm a pretty effective deterrent."

Sue was a devoted school secretary as well as the girls' volleyball coach. Her boyfriend was in a local middle-aged bar band.

Helen was getting impatient.

"Marilyn asked if, after the "Arsenic" rehearsal, I could help her pick out a safer car than the one she and Jeremy had," she said. "For her pregnancy and all."

"Do you think that's a good idea?" I said. I was maneuvering into my regular space right next to Jeremy's. His elderly, highly collectible orange Mustang was already in his spot, now Marilyn's, looking rusty and unsafe.

Helen hadn't gotten around to choosing her own car yet, what with Jeremy's disappearance and rehearsals and all. I think she liked still being driven by me, her personal chauffeur.

"She thinks I'll be able to get a good bargain on a Volvo," she said, "because I'm so assertive. See, that old wreck doesn't even have an airbag."

"But I think she suspects about you and Jeremy, Helen. What if something pops out of your mouth by mistake?"

"I don't make mistakes like that. I know exactly what I want. I want her to help me get into acting school like Jeremy said he would. I came back for a boyfriend who loves me and to get a career in the arts. I'll get the boyfriend later."

Someone rapped on my window.

"Jim wants you to go to his office after your class," Sue said, out of breath. "He just texted me."

"Has she been bad?" Helen said, smiling at us.

It was perfect timing. I could check him out as a possible sperm donor, but in a subtle way.

"Did you ever want kids?" I could say as a joke. "Probably not with all these crazy teenagers running around."

He may indeed have thought I'd been a little bad. There had been some homophobic stirrings at Bentwood about *The Color Purple* and that pesky lesbian issue. A couple of parents had called in about their daughters wearing rainbow jewelry and downloading the L-Word to their iPhones, along with sporadic girl/girl hand-holding and what one mother called a whispery relationship developing between her daughter and a best friend.

"Elizabeth, your personal life is your own, of course," Jim began, in his office after my class, twisting his hands together unpleasantly. I tried my best not to notice any of his icky mannerisms, for the good of the baby.

"For heaven's sake, Jim," I said, "I have not used literature to promote any sexual agenda if that's where you're going with this. I have no sexual agenda. Not in my class at least."

Now was clearly the time to slide into his potential sperm donation.

"Me either," he said and then to my horror he burst into tears.

I didn't know what to do. So while he dabbed at his eyes with a Kleenex from the box he kept nearby for guilty students, I looked out his window at a lovely magnolia tree and a couple of mourning doves preening themselves on one of the branches.

"It's OK," I said finally, getting up to pat him on the back. "Cry all you want. I think it's great when grown men cry."

"I shouldn't have said that," he whimpered. "There's something so empathic about you. I just don't have any luck with women. Never have had. And when you said that thing about 'sexual agenda,' I sort of lost my mind. Sometimes I think I should have been one myself."

"A woman?" I said.

"Why not? A lesbian maybe."

FROZEN

"But I thought you had issues with the Walker book."

"Not really. A few phone calls from parents I wanted to tell you about. I explained that you're a courageous, sensitive teacher who would never proselytize. That they need to give their girls space to learn about human diversity.to get That's the school theme after all."

"Wow," I said. "You're good."

"I know," he said, putting his cool glasses back on.

"Hey, Jim," I said, jumping in with a rush of that superb empathy he liked so much. "You're a good-looking guy and if I wasn't a lesbian myself, I'd go to bed with you in a flash."

He smiled so sweetly I almost believed I'd meant it.

"Then you wouldn't mind pretending to be my friend for a minute or two?" he said. "I have a special favor to ask."

He picked up the phone.

"Sue, hold all my calls would you? When's my next appointment?"

I wondered what Sue was thinking about my spending so much time with her boss.

"Want a cup of coffee?" he said after he put the phone down. "I have one of those adorable single cup machines over there." He got up and read me the labels on the coffee pods.

"Are you sure you're not gay?" I blurted out. "I haven't ever heard a straight man say the word 'adorable' in my life."

"I'm not gay. I just don't fit in anywhere. The truth is," he paused to look out the window at the magnolia tree.

"What, Jim?" I said gently. "Your secret is safe with me."

"I've never said this out loud to another person."

"I'm safe," I said again.

"I have a small penis."

Before I could stop myself I laughed at him. Then I put my hand over my mouth.

160

Had I heard him right? A small penis?

"Jim, it doesn't matter. If somebody loves you, who cares?"

"I've never even gotten that far," he said. "I'm a virgin."

"Well, I've never had actual sex with a man," I said quickly. "So there we are."

"Yes," he said. "Never mind. I needed to tell somebody and I thought you might be the one. You know, because you're gay; you're detached."

"The one?"

"I thought maybe you would hook up with me once and then I could get rid of my stupid chastity. In other words, a lesbian wouldn't really care about the size of a penis, would she?"

I gasped. I blushed. This was so perfect it was meant to be. The baby, my baby, was practically on the way.

I could hear the lunch bell ring. There was a sort of comfort in the sound as kids began to call out to each other with the joy of freedom from tight desks and fluorescent lights.

"I know it's a big favor to ask," he continued, staring at the floor. "And what would you get out of it except for an awkward and possibly painful memory? But, on the other hand, we're both single and perhaps the warmth would do us good," he paused and looked at my face almost tenderly. "At least I think you're still single."

"Yes," I said.

"So you could pretend I'm a woman, if you want."

"No, no," I said, thinking to myself that might really help.

"And I mean I'd take you to dinner or whatever you asked, or give you a gift. But to do it with a prostitute seems just too sad."

"Jim," I said, after giving him a big kiss on the cheek. "I will never love you, but I've actually been thinking along the same lines. I'm sure your penis is big enough to make me a baby. I'm ready to commit to the next generation, and I don't want to do it with some anonymous sperm bank."

"Oh wow," he said. "Oh wow. You aren't kidding, are you? You aren't making fun of me?"

"Of course not. Get me a cup of 'Daydream vanilla decaf' and let's start planning."

"You want to do it right now? The couch is actually very comfortable."

"Slow down, big guy," I said.

"But what if you're ovulating?" He jammed the coffee pod into the brewing unit with manly force.

I took a long look at him.

He had those small, almost feminine features, high cheekbones and thick curly brown hair. When we had sex I would indeed pretend he was a woman wearing a strap-on. I'd close my eyes and think about the sacrament of conception.

With his long delicate fingers, Jim handed me my cup of Daydream and I took a test sip.

"I'm always burning my tongue on these things," I said and then I blew.

"You have nice lips," he said.

"Now don't start with that," I said. "I'm a true-blue lesbian and this is a business arrangement. Not to be mean about it."

"We won't tell Helen."

For a few lovely moments I'd forgotten about her.

"If I get pregnant, she'll figure it out soon enough. When she does she'll probably kill us both."

Jim looked startled. And then I saw why. It wasn't the death threat I'd predicted; it was the sight in the magnolia tree outside his window. Helen had climbed up to the branch at eye level with Jim's office and was pretending to use binoculars to bird watch.

"How the hell did she get up there?" he said.

The binoculars fixed on us, like the barrels of a rifle.

"Helen," I shouted. "Get the hell down from there."

"What if she falls out?" Jim said, rushing to open the window. "Be careful Helen, for god's sake." He turned to me. "There could be a lawsuit."

"I wouldn't sue you over Helen. Let her fall and break her neck."

"Such a strange girl, Elizabeth. Did she come to you that way?"

"Yes," I said. "But let's not go into that now."

If I didn't jump on Jim now I might never do it. Some dangerous ideas should be acted on in the heat of the moment. Procreating with Jim in his office at Bentwood High School with my mother sitting in the tree outside his window was so absurd it was perfect.

"Close the curtains," I said. "My only rule is that we have to do it standing up."

"Why?" he said.

"So you won't go nuts and think sex with me is nice. Standing up should be just good enough to get you past your desperate status."

"Not to be too technical, but who knows if my sperm can swim upstream?"

"Good thinking," I said. "How about here instead?"

I lay down on the couch and breathed in and out a few times. I did want my baby to be made the old-fashioned way, without test tubes or turkey basters. After bringing Mom back, enough was enough with science.

On the other hand I didn't want Jim fondling my breasts or kissing my face if that could be helped.

I removed my dress and underpants while Jim unzipped his khakis. I was a flower and he was the bee. At the least, a pity fuck, a deed of good will.

I put my cheek against his.

"OK," I said. "Let's go."

He grunted. I felt his penis, like a finger, snake through my labia towards my vagina.

His breath was hot on my neck. I moaned with encouragement. And then I began to believe it. I tightened my legs together and held him close. That got him so excited he ejaculated right after he entered me.

And I had a quick and surprising orgasm.

"Shit," he said, wiping me off with the tail of his Oxford shirt.

"No matter," I said.

"Let's try it again."

"Now?" I sat up and pulled on my pants.

"No," Jim said. "Sometime when we can do it right. Not in such a hurry."

So, we looked at his office calendar and set a date when I'd probably be ovulating. But as I was leaving, my leg still sticky with his fluids, the idea of a do-over seemed unbearable.

"I'll do it better next time," he said. "I promise."

"Jim," I said with my hand on the doorknob. "This time counts. It felt just like real sex. I had an orgasm, believe it or not. My first with a guy."

"I'm applauding in my heart," he said, sheepishly.

"You are no longer a virgin, my man," I said.

That made him smile hugely which was totally worth the entire experience. He kissed me on the hand, like a true gentleman.

And at that cinematic moment the end-of-lunch bell rang. When Jim opened the curtains, Helen was gone.

I drove home smiling too. It wasn't because I'd had sex with a man, although that wasn't nearly as bad as I'd thought it would be.

The reason I was smiling was because of the baby. Even though the chances I'd gotten pregnant were just about nil, I had a glass of wine to celebrate the remote possibility with some crackers and Brie.

Then I remembered that if any of Jim's sperm were still swimming valiantly up my fallopian tubes I shouldn't be drinking alcohol. And I should also put my feet up on a big pillow to help the little fellows along. My mom told me she'd done that once after sex with my father. She'd promised him a child and had read in *Good Housekeeping* about raising the chances of conception with positive gravity flow.

The result, of course, was me.

NINETEEN

◆

"What the hell are you doing?" Helen said later, slamming the front door behind her.

It was dark. She looked at my half full glass of wine.

I sat up and rubbed my eyes.

"Celebrating something?" she asked, cutting herself a piece of Brie.

"I must have fallen asleep," I said. I looked at my watch. "What time is it?"

"Late, very late." She turned on the lights. She was wearing her school uniform but there was something wrong with it. There was something dark on the skirt.

"Where were you? With Marilyn?"

She started pacing around the living room, picking up some of the expensive bric-a-brac she'd made me take out of storage to decorate our beach house. She held a Lalique seahorse to her chest as if it was alive. Then she put it down and picked up a porcelain Lladro mermaid from the mantelpiece. She put that to her cheek. My heart stopped. She was holding these objects scarily, as if they were alive.

"Helen? What's on your skirt?"

"This has always been one of my favorites," she said. "When I was a child my grandmother gave me a present every time she came back from Europe. They traveled by ship in those days, with butlers and afternoon tea. I never went anyplace much in my last life. This time I think I'd like to go all over the world. Paris, Italy, Wimbledon. Would you go with me?"

She put down the mermaid.

There was a psycho/stagy quality to her performance that unnerved me. Mom had never been what you would call very "real," but this time she was outdoing herself as Bette Davis in a dreamy world of her own.

"Helen," I said. "Snap out of it. What's up?"

She sat down on the edge of a chair facing me. She looked terrible. Her hair was uncombed and her nose was red.

Grooming had always been one of her strong suits. Now I was really worried.

"What were you doing all that time with Jim Gibson?" she said.

"We're friends," I said.

"That figures," she said, but I could tell her thoughts were elsewhere. She began to pick at the skin on her hands the way she used to when she was old.

"Stop that," I said. "Do you want something to eat?"

She turned toward me and lit up, like she was seeing me for the first time. She began to speak rapidly, possessed.

"Now I know what you're going to think, but I swear to you it wasn't my fault. It was bad, bad luck. Terrible luck."

In spite of myself, I tried to guess, like this could still be a game.

"You were helping Marilyn pick out a car. You crashed her car. You both got out alive."

She shouted at me.

"Her goddamn fetus is dead. She crashed Jeremy's stupid Mustang without airbags into a lamppost because the accelerator got stuck."

Oh god, I thought. Helen had tampered with the car.

"How do you know the accelerator got stuck? Did you fasten it down somehow?"

"No. Why would I do that? That baby is nothing to me. I know the gas pedal got stuck because Marilyn told the police that's what it felt like. The steering wheel jammed into her gut. I was the first on the scene. I was following her home in the new Volvo. That's why I have blood on my skirt, because she was miscarrying all over the place. I pulled her out of the wreckage. I saved her life."

"Right," I said. "You paid some criminal to fuck up the accelerator pedal."

"I don't want to talk about it anymore. I'm thirsty."

I followed her into the kitchen. She tossed her skirt into the washer on the way, grabbing a bathrobe I'd folded on the dryer. It was déjà vu after the Jeremy murder.

Then she took a bottle of Perrier from the refrigerator and poured it into a Waterford goblet from the old days.

I watched her from across the room. I was afraid to get much closer.

"Could you cut me a piece of lime?" she said.

"Why didn't you call me?" I said. I reached for a lime from the fruit basket. The paring knife was so sharp I hardly had to press down on the lime to break the thick skin. How easy it would be to move it along Helen's neck and be done with all this once and for all.

"I did," she said. "Your phone was turned off, so I drove Marilyn's Volvo here from the hospital. It's in the garage. Want to see it? Want to smell the new car smell?"

"I wonder what Marilyn's going to do now?"

"She's still going to help me apply to Yale Drama School, Elizabeth. Isn't that wonderful? She thinks I have an 'enormous talent.' Her words. We talked about it while we were waiting for the paperwork on the new car."

We walked back into the living room. What else could we do?

"She told you all this while she was miscarrying?" I said.

"No, dummy, on the way to the Volvo dealer. You'll be happy to know I got Marilyn a great deal. Too bad she didn't just turn in Jeremy's car, but she wanted to keep it for sentimental reasons. Now she won't be needing the Volvo I guess."

"Why not?"

"Because it's a car for families with children." Helen looked at me steadily over the top of her crystal goblet. "I guess we should buy it from her. It could be a great deal, taking into account the depreciation just from driving it off the lot."

"What are you saying?"

I felt a light queasiness, like a golden tadpole already squirming around in my belly.

"I know what happened in Gibson's office today."

"That's impossible," I said. "You may be smart but you aren't clairvoyant."

"You might as well tell me the truth. You can't keep anything secret from me. You want a child to replace me when I go off to Yale. You think I wouldn't notice when your stomach began to pooch out?"

"How could you see anything from that tree? He closed the curtains while we did it."

"Ha, ha," she said. "Tricked you."

And that's when I realized how much power I'd attributed to Mom. She'd killed Jeremy and I let her get away with it. I assumed she'd orchestrated Marilyn's tragic accident, and now I was thinking she could see through walls.

"You devil," I said. "You don't even care that the poor woman lost her baby. I should punish you, get you sent to prison for life. It wasn't even Jeremy's child."

"Might as well have been, the way he left me for it."

"Go to your room," I said.

"Don't change the subject, Elizabeth," she said. "Don't worry. I won't kill your unborn baby. After all, she'll be my granddaughter. Blood is thicker than water."

She'd just admitted her infanticide, right to my face. I couldn't stand it.

"I'm not pregnant," I said. "How could I get pregnant in one shot? He barely entered me."

"I thought you were a lesbian," she said. "Are you still a lesbian?"

It was like she enjoyed saying the word. Over and over.

"Yes," I shouted at her. "And now I want my own damn baby."

"Oh, it just makes me sick thinking about it," she said. "You and Gibson together like that. How sad that he was your first time with a man. Promise me you won't tell your teacher's pet, Kendra. I couldn't stand the embarrassment."

"I promise." Mom always ruined everything. Not that what I'd done with Jim had been so beautiful, but still.

She began to page through a new copy of *Town and Country*, still her favorite magazine. So little had changed from the first time around. Here we were in our beautiful beach house, her reading that snobby ruling class magazine, and me apologizing for being alive.

"Isn't Princess Kate stunning? But that sister of hers is cheap. Big fat butt. Who ever heard of a name like Pippa anyway? Sounds like a cartoon rabbit."

She held up a full-page photograph of the royal family and wiggled it in my face. I could tell she was about to launch into another description of how her own mother had looked like the queen when the phone rang.

"It's Gibson," she said. "Don't answer it."

"I won't," I said, sinking down into the couch.

"Hi Elizabeth," Jim's voice boomed. "Guess I won't leave a message."

"That is a message," she said, flipping the pages and stopping abruptly at a montage of summer high society in Martha's Vineyard.

"What are you reading?" I said. Hearing Jim's eager voice so soon after our sexual encounter was pretty unnerving. I was beginning to regret the whole thing.

"I know this man," she said pointing at an enormous and lovely schooner, skippered by an old white man in a sailor suit. "It's Uncle Luther, the family banker from my old days. Stupid but rich."

She didn't seem to be interested any more in my fertility fuck with Jim, which was good. I wasn't either. I tried to think instead about Martha's Vineyard and the old days. Just in case Helen really could read my mind.

TWENTY

◆

I quit my Bentwood job the next week after handing back my students' final essays on *The Color Purple*. I mean what else did I have to teach them? That book expressed every ounce of wisdom in modern American literature.

Plus, even if Jim wanted me to take another class, there were plenty of other incentives to leave.

1. For obvious reasons, I couldn't bear to see Marilyn again.
2. Nor could I bear to greet poor Jim every time I turned around. He kept following me with a calendar and a thermometer sticking out of his pocket protector like he was my ob/gyn.
3. And then there was Helen, watching my every move at Bentwood and at home like a hungry dog, like she was already figuring out how to barbecue her grandchild once I delivered.

4. Plus, an alumna who'd actually studied literature in college had applied to be an English teacher.

Helen kept telling me to get a pregnancy test, but if I wasn't pregnant, I didn't need to know, at least not yet. For as long as I could, I wanted to keep a sweet feeling inside me, the hope that something all about me was going to happen for once in my life.

Maybe because of that, I found myself relaxing into various fantasies of murdering Mom. Nothing about her reanimation had been about me, except for my having to clean up after her wicked deeds.

Suffice it to say, the fantasies involved equipment from David's cryonics lab—which felt like poetic justice—or involved a fatal car crash, or even Mom being eaten alive by a mean and hungry giant crab.

Once the pregnancy test came back positive and I'd chosen a doctor and all of that, I stopped with the fantasies cold turkey. They say the unborn are affected by external stimuli. How much worse was the internal stuff? How could it be good for my baby to be floating around in a hot bath of my bloody matricidal impulses?

That was definitely a good side benefit of my being with child. Who knew what I'd be doing if the test hadn't worked out?

When I told Minerva, there was a long silence on the other end of the phone.

"Congratulations," she said finally. "You're breaking my heart, again."

I guess she meant because we weren't having the child together, but I didn't find out the details. She hung up right away.

When I told Helen, she shocked me by acting all excited.

"We're having a baby," she said. "How fun. I'll ask Doreen to be the nanny."

"That's a good idea," I said. We were parked in her Volvo station wagon, which she had kindly bought from Marilyn for full sticker price after Marilyn got out of the hospital. It was practically the nicest thing Mom had ever done. I still couldn't figure out exactly what was in it for her.

The expensive tiny Chinese shoes were hanging from the rear view mirror.

Helen lit a cigarette.

I didn't say a word. I opened the window instead.

"When's it due?"

"July," I said. "Right after your graduation."

Her face clouded up. I figured it had finally occurred to her the baby might be competition. She threw the cigarette out the window and turned on the motor.

"We're still going to Paris, aren't we?" she said. "You owe me that much for finishing Bentwood."

"Of course," I said. "Of course."

TWENTY-ONE

◆

Six weeks later, David walked me into the lab at Stillwaters and tossed me a pair of plastic gloves. I'd finally taken him up on his job offer, although carrying an unborn baby around a cryonics establishment was kind of rough. But, with Helen hanging around me all the time, making nasty comments about my fat stomach and my various disgusting food cravings, I knew I had to get away.

I'd liked working at Bentwood, so I figured Stillwaters would be interesting for a while. Who gets to work reanimating the dead while gestating a real fetus at the same time? There had to be a best selling memoir in it someplace. I imagined myself dictating brilliant scenes to a hired secretary while watching the waves breaking right in front of my patio.

So helping at David's while his employees were on Christmas vacation was a perfect excuse to get out of the house. Although the charming irony of a pregnant woman working to reanimate dead bodies was lost on him, he hired me temporarily.

"You're late," he said.

"Sorry," I said. "I threw up on the way over. Had to go home to change my blouse. You should try being in my state."

He was holding up a disembodied male head with a pair of heavy-duty tongs.

"I've already done the neuroseparation," he said. "I've shaved the skull and drilled the two holes required for preservation."

I quickly forgot about being nauseous. Instead I was fascinated by everything I saw.

"Roll that vat over here before I drop it," he said. "This is a very important head. It's the chairman of *Shine Time Films*. His board of directors is paying for the entire cryonic process and eventual reanimation. For now he's a silent partner. His creative gift and uncanny intuition about what audiences want is too valuable to lose to something as stupid as prostate cancer."

I rolled the vat full of foggy liquid nitrogen under the head for suspension. The guy, at fifty or sixty, hadn't been particularly good-looking but his eyes were rabbit-ish and intelligent, feral, just the way you want a movie mogul to be.

Gingerly, David put the head down in the liquid.

"Why just the head?" I asked. "Is it easier to freeze?"

"Not only that," he said. "But you don't want to know every detail of the business. Not all at once."

He gave me a couple of easy jobs and we worked together without talking for a while. When we were done, I suggested going for a walk.

David put a note on the front door of Stillwaters and we went to a nearby park.

"So what about it?" I said after we sat down on a bench.

"What about what?"

"My baby," I said.

Obviously he knew I was pregnant, but now I filled him in on the details of my brief moment of couch sex with Jim.

"If you wanted to have a baby, you should have gotten the sperm from me," he said petulantly.

"It was kind of a spontaneous decision," I said. "But, in theory, I completely agree."

"I mean, who is Jim? Some mousy little nerd high school principal who doesn't even know how to fuck."

"Be nice, David," I said, but I was kind of enjoying myself, being fought over like this. "Besides, the fact that he isn't a friend was the point. With you and me, things might have gotten messy."

"Why?"

"Well, I don't know," I said. "But I didn't want to screw up our relationship."

Actually the truth was a little different. I'd realized that I hadn't wanted to use his sperm because of the way he was associated with bringing Mom back. I wanted a baby all my own, and although Jim was her principal, he seemed more mine than hers.

I'd told Jim right away when I found out I was with child. He was beyond thrilled, even though Helen wouldn't let him in the house to see me. Not that I really minded. Right now, I wasn't planning on having Jim much in my life.

"What about Raoul?" I said to David, now.

"What about him?"

"Your relationship."

"We're OK."

"Are you happy?"

"Raoul's fine," David said. "He still gets a little on the side but not like it used to be, not like when he used to do it in my face. Besides, I've learned to look the other way. That's just the way these reanimateds are. Exaggerated."

"That's an understatement," I said. I hadn't told him my suspicions about Mom causing Marilyn's car accident and loss of Jeremy Junior. I was afraid that he'd make me do something about it.

"I'm putting him through Interment School," David continued. "He's showing an interest in the family business at last. Now I help him do his homework and he puts makeup on our clients. It works for us."

"For me, it's all been a big mistake," I said. I looked into David's big blue eyes and had a fleeting regret that I'd mated with Jim Gibson, whose eyes were brown. With David there would have been a good chance to have a baby with eyes the color of Mom's.

Then I started to cry.

"Oh, don't do that," David said, unhelpfully. He handed me a handkerchief.

I wiped my eyes.

"I'm so confused," I said. "Some days I want to kill Mom and others I want this baby to look exactly like her."

"I wish you weren't so alone," he said, which made me cry more. I mean I had Helen but that was worse than being alone and David knew it.

Then he took my hand and we watched a couple of kids playing with their parents on the grass. They were all sitting in a comfortable circle tossing a tennis ball to each other, as simple as that. Everybody was happier than hell.

"I never told you the story of my childhood, did I?" he said.

"No," I said. "I should have asked. It's been about me and Helen for all these years."

"My parents died in an accident when my sister and I were little kids," he said, gesturing toward the happy family. "About the same age as the ones over there. I told a few people once at a cryonics conference and they laughed. Can you imagine? I was the life of the cocktail party."

"Can I guess how your parents died?"

He smiled.

"You're impossible but I love you, you know," he said. "Can Raoul and I be the gay god dads?"

"They were hit by lightning," I guessed.

"No. Even worse."

"Oh my god, they were frozen."

"Bullseye," he said, giving me a high five. "They were ice skating on the pond behind our house and the surface broke through. By the time we got there all we could see was their bodies floating face up under some clear ice. I think they were dead by that time, but my sister Karen swears to this day that she could see Mom's mouth moving, calling out to us for help."

"Wow," I said. What else was there to say?

"You're not kidding," he said. We sat in silence again. Life was so heavy. I was beginning to think that the only thing that made it bearable was irony. With irony you get a little distance while you contemplate the situation.

"I'd be proud to have you and Raoul be Lizzie's god dads," I said, by way of consolation.

"Lizzie?"

"As in 'Lizzie Borden took an ax,'" I said ironically. "I just found out the baby's a girl."

"I rather like the name," he said. "But what about Jim? Shouldn't you be having this conversation with him?"

"You're my friend; he's the biological father. He keeps stopping by the house and Helen won't let him in. I don't want to see him, David. I'm afraid he'll try to share the baby."

"He's not the one you should be worrying about," he said, gravely. "Here's my cell phone. Call him up. Ask him to meet you somewhere soon.

TWENTY-TWO

◆

I did what David told me to, and then I took a walk on the beach, to give Lizzie some negative ocean ions, which the on-line New Age birthing folks promised would start her out with a mellow worldview and some happy character traits.

The seagulls and pelicans were working the waves as if they owned the whole ocean. I vowed that after this baby was delivered I'd do that too. I'd live in the moment as a natural part of the world, instead of all the time trying to force life to bend to my needs and then being afraid of the result.

David was right. I didn't know how I was going to raise my baby with Helen around. Even if she went off to drama school with Marilyn's blessing, I couldn't see how I'd ever really be rid of her. And if I wasn't ever rid of her, how could Lizzie hope to grow up right?

Three generations of badly messed up women was impossible to consider, four generations if you counted my mother living twice. Had I made a terrible impulsive mistake getting pregnant?

Gently, the tide lapped at my toes. A couple of people walked by me, talking on their cell phones or throwing a stick for their dog. A tall woman with long red hair stopped near me and silently pointed at the waves.

"Dolphins," I said. They were frolicking, three of them, as if they didn't have a care in the world, as if plastic garbage bags, tuna nets or outboard motors and oil spills weren't lying in wait.

"They're so beautiful," the person said. I turned and looked at her. She was a woman who looked like a man or vice versa, wearing a batik sarong and a short sleeved blouse. His voice was deeper than you'd expect for a woman, but she had breasts and that long hair. Not somebody you'd expect to run across on our little beach at dusk.

"Elizabeth, it's me, Jim," the gal said when I turned to walk on.

I've found that when people are acting strangely, sometimes it's best to look past it. So instead of asking him why he was dressed as a woman, I said,

"What are you doing here?"

"I thought I'd give you a big surprise."

"This costume is supposed to be a joke?"

He twirled around and around so I could see both sides of his outfit, which wasn't all that easy to do with bare feet in the sand. He looked sad and absurd, like a hippie girl version of Bozo the clown. He had to put a hand on top of his head to keep the red wig from flying off into the waves.

He had a rattan beach bag over his shoulder and gold espadrilles in his left hand, shoes that he must have special ordered.

"How do I look?"

His voice was so vulnerable and pleading I couldn't answer.

"I'm meeting you at the beach like you said. I'm here to court you."

"I told you long ago I'm not into men," I said, and then the outfit and the hair hit me.

"I've decided to come out as a person with gender dysphoria," he said happily. "I thought if I became a woman, you might be able to love me. We could make a family."

"Oh Jim," I said. "That's not the way it works."

Crazy as it sounds, he warmed my heart. Jim was willing to change his gender just for me.

"How do you know?" he said, pushing his regular round frames back onto the bridge of his nose. His face was sweating probably from all the extra hair on his head. He was trying so goddamn hard.

A golden retriever ran to us and dropped her ball at Jim's feet. He picked it up and threw it half the length of the beach. The baby would have good coordination, that was for sure.

"Nice toss," the owner said, looking at Jim quizzically.

After he left, Jim seemed to deflate.

"I'll never pass," he said. "That man knew I was a guy right away."

"Of course lots of women have a strong throwing arm," I said, "but it's still a bit unusual. And some men can't throw at all."

"I have a small penis," he said, with desperate conviction, tossing his wig onto the sand. "God obviously made a mistake and I'm going to fix it. I just won't throw balls."

"Don't worry. I'll share this baby with you," I said. I felt so bad for him I just had to make things OK. "No need to resort to surgery. I've learned the hard way; nobody can get away with playing God."

"What do you mean?"

"Like changing your gender or your appearance. Your age. Lots of things."

"Who are you to judge?" he shouted, finally in his real man-voice. "There are plenty of transsexuals more successful than you or me. Look at Chaz. Look at Renee Richards and Jan Morris. How dare you be so insensitive to another person's pain?"

"Come with me," I said. "We need to talk."

I led him to the public restroom and told him to put on his regular clothes, which he'd brought in his bag. Without a word, he went into the men's side. I think he was relieved that I didn't like his idea.

In as a woman and out as a man.

"Well," he said, wearing his regular beige chinos and green golf shirt.

"Feel better?" I said.

"Yes," he said.

We sat down at a picnic table.

I'd never talked to Minerva or any other girlfriends in the soul baring kind of way I was about to with Jim. And with David too, all on the same day. Maybe I'd been this honest with my therapist but that wasn't exactly real. How stupid is it to pay somebody to listen to lies?

Women were harder because with some of them I actually had something to lose. Now, I had to tell Jim all the truth. Why? Because he deserved it.

And also because Lizzie was giving me a good swift kick from the inside out.

"Ouch," I said.

"Let me feel," he said.

I put my hand over his and moved it over my stomach. And then I told him everything I could.

TWENTY-THREE

◆

"Come swimming, come swimming. I've got a little place with a pool. It's good for pregnant women to float," Doreen called me to say, after Mom told her the news.

I promised her she'd be the first on my list as a nanny.

Minerva was angry the next time I saw her. Big surprise. She thought we should have been co-parents.

"You could have saved me from having all these subsequent ridiculous relationships. I could have had a normal stable life with depth and children, with you."

"Oh gosh, Min, I never thought of it that way," I said.

We'd run into each other in the after-school pick up line where I was waiting for Helen. Her (formerly Marilyn's) Volvo was getting serviced.

Minerva and I parked our cars and were sitting down on some grass by the flagpole to wait for Kendra and Helen, who'd announced that they still had half an hour to put in at detention. Helen was being punished for Tardies, uniform violations and a little bit of back talk in social studies.

Kendra, who'd merely been late to school one time too many, thought Helen's bad behavior was funny.

The Social Studies teacher didn't agree, so although you couldn't give out demerits for students' stupid right wing political positions, he found other stuff like untied sneakers or forgetting to bring the US history text to class. I didn't really blame him. I understood the need to release some of the rage Mom brought out in people.

Minerva was now giving me the silent treatment as if I still somehow was making her life a victim of mine. She picked out the clover in the lawn and was fussing with it like she was trying to make fairy garlands or wedding rings. I could tell she was nerved up being with me.

"Boy or girl?" she asked finally.

"Girl," I said.

"Lucky," she said. "You'd be terrible with a boy."

What she'd said made no sense, but I let it go. She would have said the same thing in reverse if I'd told her I was having a boy.

I looked at her. She was so lovely but so needy, too. I remembered falling for her dusky good looks and making up the rest of it, character, intelligence, personality and wit. It's amazing what you can do after you sleep with somebody in order to make sense out of continuing the relationship.

In addition, she was always telling me to open up, to talk about my feelings as if knowing me better would make us close. As if there was more to know.

Clearly, I was all mixed up. But I'd never tell her that. I knew just where'd she go with it, back to the two of us being perfect together.

"So who's the father?" she asked, tossing the wad of clover at my stomach.

"You don't know? Helen didn't tell Kendra?"

"Anonymous sperm donor is what she said."

"She must have been embarrassed," I said.

"Why?" Minerva asked, at which moment the answer came leaping toward us, slipping and then sliding across the wet lawn on his butt, laughing and yelping like a puppy the whole time. Jim was, depending on your taste, either adorable or ridiculous. Minerva, I'm sure, thought he was a total joke.

"Elizabeth and Kendra's mom, hi," he said, standing up and wiping the backside of his cords. "Jim Gibson, principal, although we've met several times and you undoubtedly know that."

He held out his dirty hand to shake Minerva's.

"My name's Minerva," she said. "You have nice small hands."

Jim blushed hugely, as if she was mistakenly describing his penis.

She looked at me and then at him. And at that moment Minerva realized that the principal was Lizzie's dad.

"Yep," I said. "It's true."

"Oh wow," she said and then, "So it's almost like Jim and I are related."

Luckily, she didn't go into the details of what she meant.

TWENTY-FOUR

◆

I felt so calm when Dr. Wolf listened to my belly and then when he showed me the ultrasound of my little girl.

He never asked me a bunch of details about my partner, husband, family, whatever. They probably taught you in modern medical school to avoid stereotyped expectations of pregnant women under your care.

Maybe everybody fell for their obstetrician. He was different from what you'd expect a male doctor to look like. He was big and brawny, more like an ex-linebacker, with big hairy blond arms and a head shaved bald. He was a bit younger than me and in great shape, as if he worked out all the time when he wasn't catching newborns falling from their mothers' wombs.

"You work out?" I asked at my second visit, after he'd carefully, almost tenderly listened to my heart.

"My wife and I work out together," he said, washing his hands. "She used to be a competitive bodybuilder, but now she teaches in a gym she owns. People like her inspire me—people who are completely connected to their bodies. Maybe that's why I became a doctor. Does that make sense?"

"Yes, I understand," I said. There was a connection between the brain and body. There had to be. And Dr.Wolf wanted to bring them together. He was always telling me to listen to good music and meditate when I had time. For the baby.

It was something I'd never thought about, but it did make sense. In my life, all I'd really emphasized was Mom's body, how it was sad and dwindling when she got old and how it was growing more beautiful now that she was young. How, for some reason, she of all people had gotten two lives.

Having a baby inside me was changing all that in a good way. With Lizzie's help, I was beginning to start considering myself.

Then the female nurse came in as Dr. Wolf began the internal exam. I held my breath and smiled.

Another good thing about carrying a baby was that I always felt warm and full of life. And because I'd told Jim Gibson everything about Mom (except her murders of Jeremy and Jeremy Junior, which would have been asking way too much of his powers of empathy) I had my own full-blown support system of one.

David and Raoul were nice to me when they had time, but their work on the expansion of Stillwaters made them pretty unreliable. They were always having complicated meetings about contracting for or accepting mysterious equipment deliveries.

Except when she was jealous, Helen pretty much ignored me. And, even though she was living with Kendra's dad, Frank, again, Minerva was still blaming me for what she called the charred ruin of her life.

But I'd lucked out with Jim. He was the best. We often lay on my big bed side by side, fully clothed, because that's where I wanted to be most of the time. I'd quit Stillwaters because of swollen ankles, which I now kept raised on a couple of my firmest pillows.

Today Jim was describing his mother and the stories she'd told him about her family in Missoula, Montana–a bunch of strong women who built their own wood houses at age 70–things like that. Jim liked powerful women. He even liked Helen.

"Hey there, Helen, my woman," he said when she came into the bedroom after returning from her once a week volunteer job at the hospital that Bentwood required as community service.

She plopped down between us in her striped pink uniform and sighed. Sometimes she even tried to push Jim off the bed, but today she wasn't into competing for attention. Evidently she'd gotten enough.

"The sick and dying just love me," she said. "Several of them have added me to their list of beneficiaries. It's frowned upon, but what can the hospital administrators do if old men with congestive heart failure want to send me to their alma mater? Yale School of Drama, Harvard, Oxford in England?"

"What a vixen you are," Jim said. "I bet you were a cougar in your first life. You probably seduced the pool boy when you were seventy."

Jim tried hard to use words like "cougar" so he could relate to his students about television and social media. I found it kind of charming.

"We didn't have a pool," she said. "We had a private beach, like now."

Helen still didn't like Jim, of course, partly because he was the principal and now because I'd decided to give him some claim to the baby. Too bad. They had quite a bit in common with the body dysphoria: Mom, an old lady in a girl's body and Jim always with that small penis issue of his.

"Just a metaphor," he said. "You know. Pool boy, gardener, tennis pro."

"I get it," she said. She thought Jim was dorky, a nothing, as she put it and she wanted him out of our life, the sooner the better.

Her big dream was still the three of us girls in Paris for a year, Lizzie, Helen, and me, creating Left Bank memories and shopping for a closet full of fashion before she moved on to drama school or whatever. Probably also an older French boyfriend whose heart she could break over a Gauloise and glass of absinthe.

"Why does she dislike me so?" Jim said after she left. "Doesn't she know I won't be taking you or Lizzie away from her?"

"Who knows what she's thinking," I said. "The most I understand is that everything's supposed to be about her."

"Well, I'll try not to make too big a fuss over the baby, and I know you won't ever make a fuss over me." He patted my puffy ankles affectionately.

That was the best thing about him, I decided then and there. He was the opposite of my mother. Jim would be astounded if you picked him out of a line up; Helen would be shocked if you didn't.

She reappeared in her nightgown, a childish Lanz flannel number she'd found somewhere all covered with yellow duckies and red and blue rainbows. Pedophiles would have drooled.

"Bye, bye, Jim. Time to go home," she said, slipping under the covers with me. "You big dork."

"I love you anyway," he said and then he left.

"Now what was that supposed to mean?" she said. She looked as surprised as I'd ever seen her and either moved or upset or both. An actual tear formed in the corner of her eye. Sure, she expected people to adore her, but not so much after she'd spent all her energy insulting them.

Probably, in the long run, it made her hate him even more.

TWENTY-FIVE

◆

The baby arrived so easily I'd almost have to say she came to me on a cloud. The natural contractions were more like breezy dreams than the hot torture I'd heard about. Jim had seen me through birthing classes, so I'd learned how to breathe and push.

That's the way I like to remember it.

Actually, the natural birth thing was the most difficult experience I'd ever been through. Breaking my arm, terrible menstrual cramps, bleeding hemorrhoids, were nothing compared to having Lizzie.

But, somehow I figured the pain was worth it to make it real, unlike Mom's reanimation, which happened like magic. The ripping, tearing, burning endless shock of pain cleaned my spirit.

Helen thought the whole natural childbirth thing was stupid.

"Just go to sleep," she'd advised me. "Wake up with a nice and neat baby in your arms—no stink, no pain. You wouldn't want to associate your baby with pain, would you? You're too old to go without anesthesia."

But Dr. Wolf expressed pride at my limber delivery, telling me I gave birth with the ease of a younger, more experienced woman.

I was proud, but not about that. I was proud of how brave I'd been in order to have my baby the way I wanted her.

The best part was when Jim put Lizzie on my chest. I looked into the eyes of my beloved, and for the first time in years I didn't see Mom looking back. I saw my own little brown-eyed girl who depended on me and would love me uncritically, at least for a while.

"She's so beautiful," I said tearing up.

Jim wept a little bit, too.

Dr. Wolf wouldn't let Helen into the room until after the delivery. He said she was too young, but I'm sure he could tell she was trouble.

Which became pretty obvious once she started pounding on the door.

"Let her in," I said, sighing.

"It took you long enough," she said, pushing Jim out of the way to take Lizzie.

"Careful, dear," the nurse said, watching her carefully.

"I know how to hold a baby," Helen said, although I couldn't remember her doing it ever, with me or with anybody else.

"Look at her eyes," I said.

"Why are they brown?"

"Because of us," I said, in three words creating an entirely new and separate family unit. Jim, Lizzie and me.

"What?" Helen said, her cheeks suddenly all red.

I tried to cover it.

"I meant her eyes are so bright it's like she's looking at you."

"She can't see a thing," Helen said. "She's blind as a bat. Maybe they'll turn blue if we're lucky."

"Oh," I said. For once I didn't care how mean she was.

All I felt was free. The truth is suddenly Mom didn't matter much to me anymore. I had to pretend she did, of course, or who knew where her temper would take her?

She could tell things had changed.

"She looks just like I did," she said, "except for the eyes."

Which I figured was a good thing.

To keep Helen happy while I was pregnant I'd let her have sleepovers with this perfectly ridiculous massage therapist she met on-line. Secretly I also hoped she'd direct all her free-floating anger at the new boyfriend, Kai, like she had with Jeremy, although obviously not in such an extreme and bloody way.

Luckily, Lizzie didn't cry much, which could have spelled trouble with Mom; she had nothing to complain about there. And, as in her first life with me as the baby, never ever did she have to lift a finger now that I had Doreen to help me during the day.

While Helen finished up physics at summer school so she could get a diploma, Lizzie and I got to be alone, often rocking in front of the big picture window. She'd look at me when I nursed her and I became the only person in the world. I loved her so much I thought my heart would break.

Mom, of course, thought nursing was disgusting.

"You look like an animal," she said whenever she saw me doing it. "A pig or a goat. You were bottle-fed formula by the nanny and you came out fine. Yuck. You can't enjoy that."

Usually she'd turn and go to her room or someplace else, but today, after play rehearsal, she just stood next to us and stared. I looked out the window at the waves breaking on the shore and tried to pretend she wasn't there. When Lizzie was finished I patted her back until she burped.

I figured I'd better say something to Helen so she wouldn't feel neglected and pissed off.

"You want to hold your granddaughter, Mom?"

I'd asked her plenty of times before, hoping the touch and smell of Lizzie would help Mom to bond, but she'd never taken me up on it.

Today, for some reason, she thought about it.

"OK," she said finally. "Make sure she doesn't spit up."

She sat down on the couch and held out her arms. Lizzie nuzzled into her chest, like she was still hungry.

"It's just instinct," I said.

"See, I'm right," Mom said. "Just like an animal." She held onto Lizzie anyway, almost as if she liked it.

"Never mind," I said, reaching out to take her back. But Helen was already unbuttoning her Bentwood blouse and pulling up her bra.

"Don't do that," I said.

"I want to see what the big attraction is," she said. "What it feels like."

"It's about the nutrition in mother's milk," I said. "She's not a sex toy."

"Ouch," she said, jamming the baby's mouth on her nipple.

"Give her to me." This was so crazy. I was about to grab the baby from her like a mother in front of King Solomon.

"OK, OK," she said, handing Lizzie back. "Her mouth hurt me. Even without teeth. Can I taste the milk?"

"No," I said.

I couldn't help but wonder how the hell I was going to live with her in my life much longer, how I could stop myself from seeing her as a creepy parasite. Mostly I tried to repress and deny but at times like this, I felt all this poisonous rage. My milk probably tasted like bile.

Luckily, Doreen made a charming daytime companion. Who knew? After all those years taking care of Mom, I'd worried about us getting along, but things went as smooth as snow.

She helped me with Lizzie but not in an overbearing way, and she did all the extras too, like cleaning and laundry. When Helen got home from school, they'd usually spend some cozy time together over cookies homemade by Doreen, but I didn't mind. As long as Helen was defanged, happy, and all of that.

For their first viewing, David and Raoul came over one Sunday with balloons and a cake. I could tell their hearts weren't in it. They didn't look at Lizzie very long and not once at each other, except when they took the cake into the kitchen to cut. That's when I heard them fighting.

"Don't listen," Helen said.

"You're kidding. Why not? You're telling me to behave?"

"Hush," she whispered, listening herself.

"You're a greedy S.O.B.," we could hear David say. "You're going to close us down and then what? You're way too old to turn tricks."

Sound of a slap.

Sound of a plate breaking.

"Don't worry," Raoul called out to us. "It's our plate, the one we brought the cake on. We'll sweep it up."

Lizzie started to cry.

In a few minutes, on a new plate, David brought in the pretty white cake with pink and yellow bears prancing on the top. He was making a grand uneven attempt to smile. Raoul brought up the rear with the serving stuff, looking pale. I noticed that David's cheek was still red where his boyfriend had slapped his face.

Lizzie stopped crying.

"Can she have a little cake?" David asked. "It's to celebrate her birth."

"Don't you know anything about babies?" Helen said. "She's breast feeding for god's sake."

Raoul blushed. That was strange.

"No, Helen, we don't know a thing about babies," David said, looking significantly at Raoul. "Neither of us."

They were hiding something, that was for sure, and I didn't have the extra energy to find out what it was.

"It doesn't matter," I said, taking a little bit of the frosting on my finger and offering it to Lizzie. Her first real food.

"Who cares?" Helen said and then she cut herself a big piece and bit in.

"Pretty good, " she mumbled with her mouth full of the stuff.

The rest of the visit was uneventful and mildly unpleasant. It made me sadder than usual to be with them, sadder even than right after Raoul came back, all angry and ungrateful. I couldn't understand why they stayed together. At least with Helen I had a reason to keep our relationship workable. If I didn't, I was afraid she'd kill me or Lizzie, or both of us at once.

TWENTY-SIX

◆

At 6:45 the next evening when I got David's frantic phone call, I was holding Lizzie on my lap while running Helen through her lines in *Macbeth*. She was in the summer drama club even though the new coach, the one who had taken Marilyn's place after she returned to television in New York City, was a fat, middle-aged female recently retired from low budget horror films. Helen still hated fat people and most women, too, but I'm sure she would have liked horror films if she'd been exposed to the genre.

They were right up her alley.

Macbeth seemed like a strange choice for the hot days of July, but Helen had insisted that they do it and she evidently still had some clout.

I followed the lines as she spoke them.

" If it were me, I would have taken the nursing babe from my nipple and bashed its head against the wall."

"Close enough," I said to her. It was the place where Lady Macbeth was trying to shame her husband into killing the king. Helen was doing a great job even though her line recall wasn't perfect. I, of course, wouldn't let her use Lizzie as a prop.

"Big emergency," David said, his voice shaking like mad. All I could hear were the sounds of giggling and splashing behind him. Was he at the gay baths or what?

"Are you at Stillwaters?" I said. "Sounds more like a little kid's birthday party."

"Stillwaters," he said. "We need your help right now."

I'd been there until my last trimester, so I knew all the ropes.

"What do you need?"

"What's he saying?" Helen asked.

"Just get over here."

"I'll have to bring Lizzie," I said.

"Absolutely not," David said. "I don't want her to see this. Even if it's only going to be a subliminal memory."

And then he hung up.

Doreen wasn't picking up her cell phone, and Jim was out of town at a principals' conference, so I did a terrible thing. I took a chance and left my helpless baby alone with Helen. David sounded so desperate.

"She's asleep in her crib," I said as I left. "Only pick her up if she starts crying. I'll be back in an hour. And remember, I love you most."

"Don't worry," Helen said, sniggering wickedly. "I'm not going to hurt her if that's what you're worried about. She's a blood relation. I told you that. I have to draw the line somewhere. Besides I have better things to do. I have to learn *Macbeth*."

Fifteen minutes later I walked into a nightmare I never could have imagined. It was even worse than the murder of Jeremy.

"What is this?" I said, putting my hand over my mouth. Imagine the smell of chlorine and rotting garbage. Sweet and pungent. And air that was thick and wet, like a budget spa where people wore dirty towels around their sweaty waists.

I entered Raoul's new addition to the reanimation area where a large plastic swimming pool was full of water and eight or ten naked babies paddling with delight. Around the edges of the room were another half dozen infant bodies lying motionless on blue beach towels. And finally, in the corner, wearing a filthy gray sweatshirt was Raoul, empty coffee cups littering the floor around him.

"Here," David said, handing me a shuddering infant he'd just scooped from the pool. "Introducing Harriet Huntington. She's about to age eighty years in your arms. And then she'll die. Comfort her as best you can."

I grabbed a towel from the stack near Raoul and swaddled the infant.

"Thank you," he muttered. He looked awful. There was stubble on his face and his bloodshot eyes had big dark bags under them. He kept rocking himself.

I sat in a folding chair and tried to soothe Harriet as best I could, given the fact that her little body and round face were wrinkling up right before my eyes.

She began to whimper.

She reminded me of Lizzie, which made it a lot worse.

"Help," she moaned, rolling her baby head back and forth on my arm.

"Help," I called to David who was busy playing with the rest of the babies splashing around in the shallow pool.

"Nothing else we can do," he said, coming over to me.

"What happened?" I said. I suddenly realized that this new moneymaking scheme must have been what their argument in my kitchen had been about.

"Raoul's greed got insatiable and I, stupidly, went along with him." David bent his head in shame. "I'd still do anything to keep him."

"What did he need the money for?"

"Just things," he said. "Nothing really. A gold Rolex, a tummy tuck, probably gifts for one or two boyfriends. Money substituting for youth, sex, whatever. Those ugly out-of-control side effects we discussed."

"Like Mom and murder?" I said.

I thought about her at home with Lizzie and shivered.

"But what's going on?" I asked him again. I had to help him fast and get out of there to my own baby.

"When he got so badly into debt he told me about this foolproof procedure he'd read about. Three days ago he regressed all our clients to infancy for twice the regular reanimation fee. We didn't know infancy stimulates a rapid-aging response as soon as they tire of swimming. But, Elizabeth, it changed him. He's been up for two days trying to reverse the process."

"It's no use," Raoul said from the corner of the room. "They just shrivel up and die. Harriet Huntington was a railroad engineer, one of the first women. Her partner read about us in the newspaper while Harriet was dying of congestive heart failure. She trusted me to give them another life together, and now look at what I've done."

"There's no antidote," David said. "We have to see them through. It's our sacred duty for bringing them here, to this horror."

Just then Harriet sighed deeply and loosened her grip on my finger.

"She's gone," I said and placed her on the floor, now an empty husk.

A moment later, David handed me Tom Gosnell, a retired banker who'd broken his neck skiing.

Everybody was dead in an hour, and by then Raoul had recovered enough to place them in several plastic garbage bags for removal. Then the three of us held hands and said a prayer to the natural order of things, which we had all defied in one way or another.

It was so huge a moment that I truly began to believe Raoul might be coming back to his old self. And if he could recover from an age-manipulated character disorder, could Helen?

But right away I remembered that even if she never murdered anybody again, there was nobody any good for her to turn back into.

So that ended that line of thinking, and then we were driving David's Stillwaters van packed with the dead babies heading for Fletcher's field, a kind of place where kids lit fires and stoned stray dogs to death.

We needed to get rid of the corpses.

David had first offered the dissolution tank, but Raoul had refused.

"This is my problem that you shouldn't have to solve," he said. "I don't want you thinking about these babies every time you go to work."

"You have to stop bringing anybody back at any age," I managed to say. "Give the frozen bodies to another cryonics place and tell the relatives you're opening a restaurant."

"After our doctor examined these babies and saw there was nothing he could do, he split," Raoul went on as if I hadn't said a word, as if he was in another world. "I don't know what

I would be doing now without you both. You are my closest people in the world."

David looked at me to make sure I got the point. There was hope for Raoul.

"Thanks," I said, "but I've left an innocent real baby at home with my monster, unchaperoned. Let's get going."

Right then we heard a baby whimper from the back of the truck.

"We must have missed one," I said.

"Get it out; maybe we can save it," Raoul said.

"We can't," David said putting his hand on Raoul's thigh. "It will all be over soon."

After the last baby died we dragged the bags out of the truck past cactus, Joshua trees, rusted cars, unidentifiable bones and bedsprings.

We piled paper and leaves around the edges of the baby mound and Raoul covered the whole thing with lighter fluid we'd picked up at a 7-ll.

I turned away from the burning bodies and called home.

Helen answered after four rings. Lizzie was screaming in the background.

"Is she OK?" I said. My stomach turned over.

"Of course," she said. "We're playing hide and seek."

"You can't play hide and seek with an infant," I screamed. "She'll be terrified."

"I put her in the corner of your bedroom," she said. "I'm going to find her in a couple minutes. I need a time out."

Just then I began to hear a new awful popping sound from the baby fire. Would it never end?

"What's that?" she said.

"What's that?" I shouted to David.

"It's the sound of various organ sacks exploding," he said. I relayed the whole story to Helen.

"Sounds like an awesome bonfire," she said. "Can I come?"

"No," I said firmly. "It's almost over anyway. Pick up Lizzie now and read her *Goodnight Moon.* I'll be home in a few minutes."

"Take a picture with your phone then," she said. I'm ashamed to say that I did and sent it to her right away.

Fifteen minutes later I got my car at Stillwaters and drove home as fast as I could. After watching all those babies die, I couldn't help but visualize Lizzie's little body lifeless on the hallway floor or smothered in some closet. Why I left her with Helen I'll never know.

Minerva and Kendra met me at the front door.

"Why did you leave the baby alone with Helen?" Min said sternly. She'd obviously had a shock. Her face was gray and her hands were shaking like mad.

As I rushed to the crib, I yelled toward Helen's room, "If you hurt her, I'll kill you."

Lizzie was sleeping. For the second time in the last couple of hours, I wanted to weep.

I leaned over her mouth. Her soft breath moistened my cheek.

"Jeez," Helen said, standing behind me. "I didn't touch her. Min just gave her some baby sleep medicine so she wouldn't cry. I don't know how you stand it."

Minerva had saved Lizzie's life. I had no doubt about it. Finally I began to cry.

"I called Helen to help me with this stupid love sonnet the teacher assigned," Kendra said. "And she told me Lizzie was driving her nuts. So I got my mom to drive us over."

Evidently Kendra was seeing the real Helen, too.

I took the baby into my arms and silently forgave Minerva for everything I'd ever held against her. Lizzie watched me peacefully and then went back to sleep. We sat down in the rocking chair and I wiped my eyes.

I'd never cried much in front of Helen except maybe once or twice in frustrated rage. Now it was from pure relief.

"You do love her more than you love me," she said.

I'd never seen her face so angry before, even when I was a kid and had the stupidity to talk back. Her eyes were hard slits and her mouth was pinched tight.

"I love you differently," I said quickly.

Then I yawned deeply. I was surprisingly calm. My baby was safe.

"So I guess we'll get going," Minerva said, patting my back. Kendra kissed me on the cheek.

"At least you got a good sonnet out of it," Helen said to her pal. "Want to hear the beginning, Elizabeth?"

I nodded, in a fog.

Kendra pulled it out of her binder and began to read:

"True love is more than just having wild sex,

Sometimes it means getting back with your ex."

"Kendra," Min snapped.

"Helen wrote it," Kendra said. "She dictated it."

"Who cares?" Helen said. "I meant Min and Frank, your dad, obviously. If they break up again. Not you two. Not Elizabeth and Min. Ick."

TWENTY-SEVEN

◆

OK, so I knew it was time to make my peace with Minerva. Not only was my heart too full of disgust with Mom for me to raise Lizzie with anything close to calm affection, but here I was also dragging the baggage of my complicated disdain for Minerva, like a rotten dead animal, without even the help of a stroller.

So when the three of us, Mom, me and Lizzie, walked by the "absolutely adorable" tea place on the edge of the upscale Fashion Mall that Mom loved and saw Min and Kendra eating crumpets, I had to stop.

"Join us," Kendra said, reorganizing the seating and lace doilies.

Lizzie was asleep in the stroller David and Raoul had given her. Mom, although she'd recently dismissed Kendra as a prissy oreo with a heart of steel, knew a good shopping partner when she saw one.

This is where their relationship had begun, after all.

FROZEN

"Whoa," Min said, smirking. "So you're going to grace us with your presence?"

Helen and Kendra glanced at us.

"Let's go, Helen," Kendra said. "There's that new Forever 21 with 20% off behind Tiffany's."

They skipped off, and Minerva poured me some tea into Kendra's empty cup."

"Do you mind using hers?" she said.

"Nope," I said and took a sip.

I smelled it first and then took a gulp.

It was some strange flavor: hibiscus and roots, or it could have been rose petals and rice water.

"Sip it," Min said. "It tastes better that way. It's supposed to be good for your heart."

I sipped. It tasted better.

Then I took a tiny heart-shaped egg sandwich from the tiered tray to my left.

"Delicious," I said.

Between us, in her stroller, Lizzie began to wake up, stirring, her arms outstretched, not crying, thank the lord.

"May I hold her?" Minerva said, putting down her cup.

"Sure."

I watched them together, Lizzie reaching up to Min's mouth, Min kissing her fingers lightly with her full lips.

"She's a beautiful baby," she said and I noticed there were tears in her eyes. "She looks like you."

"Oh god, I hope not," I said. "My big nose, my pink skin. Now if she was yours, she'd be so pretty."

Minerva rubbed her cheek on Lizzie's head so gently, so, well, maternally, that I almost reached out and touched her arm.

Her eyes were still full of tears.

And then I realized what I'd said.

"I'm sorry, Min."

"I still don't understand why we couldn't have done this when we were together." She put the baby back in the stroller and began to move it slowly back and forth.

"It was something about my mother," I said, taking a tiny cucumber and cream cheese on white. "I started to dream about having something of my own, something that wasn't a monster."

"You could have had me."

I looked at her, really looked. And, with her clear green eyes, Minerva looked right back. It made me shiver.

"You keep saying that, but how could you really want me?" I said, a little too loud. "I'm ugly; I'm so mean to you; I disdain you for loving me; I spit on you behind your back."

"You can't help it," she said quietly.

The couple to our right, two older women, glanced at us and then went back to pouring their tea.

"I keep treating you like shit," I said.

"Just like your mother treated you."

I tried to let that sink in but I couldn't hold on to it. Sometimes those great insights drift on by. They're too big.

"How can you love somebody like me?" I continued. "You must be some kind of masochist. I'm nothing. Nothing."

I could feel my face getting red and sweaty. Something was happening inside me.

"I see you," Min said softly. "Your mother never did. I see you all the way through."

"But I'm fat," I shouted, pulling hard on the flesh of my upper arm, as if I could yank all the skin off if I tried hard enough.

"Stop," she said. And then she did the best thing. She picked up her cup and tossed all her warm tea into my face.

With the shock of that, I melted.

Lizzie started to wail, and the manager asked us to leave. I took Min's hand and both of us pushed Lizzie out.

TWENTY-EIGHT

◆

That baby-sitting incident combined with the horror of the dying reanimated infants inspired me to repeat my ultimatum to David and Raoul: Close down Stillwaters completely or I will report you to the authorities. No more crazies getting reanimated and then acting out their freshly uninhibited dark sides. No more murdering Moms or sex-crazed Raouls.

Besides, who knew what other evil was going on out there in the netherworld of unfrozen souls? I couldn't stop all the rape, theft, wife-battering and dog abuse they'd probably unleashed, but, after stopping R and D, at least there wouldn't be an endless new population of cryonic cases embarking on a second, frequently nasty, life.

At first they refused, of course. It wasn't my business, and Mom was the only bad seed they'd ever heard of, except for Raoul, who luckily was all-better now.

They then proceeded to cite all sorts of lovely cryonic success stories: the dead soldier who was able to raise his orphaned kids (under an assumed name of course), the old research scientist who came back to discover the cure for ALS (they swore the news would be out soon). Best of all was the failed screenwriter who, after dejectedly committing suicide, returned to write a hit Broadway play about lesbians changing the world, a sort of Lysistrata for the 21st century.

I couldn't prove whether any of the stories were true, but, in spite of that, they almost moved me enough to back down.

Luckily, all it took to strengthen my resolve was watching Helen on the Bentwood Summer Stage as a freakishly believable Lady Macbeth. Her best acting came when she used humiliation and emotional blackmail to manipulate her weak consort into killing the king.

"Yet I do fear thy nature is too full of the milk of human kindness to catch the nearest way. Were you a man when you first told me this?"

"She's very good," Raoul said during intermission. "It's kind of scary."

"Perfect pacing," David said. "You can tell she's lived one full life already from the depth of her portrayal of evil."

"Yeah, right," I said. "She's hardly acting at all. She is evil. And what you guys are doing is, too."

Wow, speaking up felt so good. With Helen, I was still much too afraid of her potential impulses toward infanticide to set any decent limits.

But now, maybe I was actually going to save a few lives if the boys took me seriously and shut down their cryonics business.

David and Raoul looked at me for a long time. Then, evidently speechless, they left without watching the rest of the show. I guess everybody knows what happens at the end. Lady

Macbeth just sort of faded into madness while Macbeth let the witches take over his life.

A few months later Waterfall, David and Raoul's new restaurant, opened, taking over the building Stillwaters and Aquarium had occupied. It sported a huge waterfall at one end of the room where the frozen bodies used to be held in their temperature-controlled beds. This in turn fed a freshwater pond stocked with fish. The heartier patrons were allowed to catch their own.

David and Raoul invited Helen and me to the opening and were gracious as hell. During the presentation of a puffy pink crab amuse bouche, David whispered "thank you" into my ear.

So that intervention went all right.

But Helen was another issue altogether.

In March of her senior year, when I'd promised her that trip to Paris if she graduated with all A's and B's, I figured it was reasonable enough to keep her from retaliation if she couldn't pull it off.

Which is where summer school physics came in. I allowed her that wiggle room just to keep the peace. And, after all, what harm could come from a month on the Left Bank?

I was pretty certain Jim would be in for the adventure once I told him our plans. It was only fair to include him. He could take a brief sabbatical from Bentwood to bond with us.

And honestly, it felt safer to have another person to watch what Helen had up her sleeve.

Of course, she could have just gone off with the newest boyfriend, a dark-haired pastry chef named Nick, to share a romantic attic on the Left Bank. But, all her life she'd needed somebody to take care of her, and I guess a young foodie boyfriend couldn't be counted on to do that.

Or else she wanted to keep an eye on me and Lizzie to assure herself of a place in my life. It wasn't love, of course—more like the need to possess. She'd always been greedy that way, about objects and people. They were interchangeable.

I knew she'd hate the idea of taking Jim with us but it seemed only fair to include him in the family adventure.

I didn't worry so much about Helen wanting to kill Lizzie any more. She actually changed the baby's diapers without complaint and sometimes even rocked her to sleep, singing Frère Jacques in her sweetest voice.

I may not have worried exactly, but I didn't leave the baby at home without Doreen there, too. Just in case her mood changed.

"Helen," I said one weekend at lunch, after the two of us shared a bacon and mushroom quiche Nick, the surprisingly good boyfriend, had brought over for us the night before. "There's something we need to talk about."

"God, we have the cutest, nicest, smartest baby, don't we, Elizabeth?" She was bite/kissing Lizzie's cheeks for dessert.

Lizzie, luckily, was a placid, trusting infant so she never pushed Helen away. She'd obviously inherited those pleasant traits from Jim, not either of us, so right there was another argument for the existence of God.

"Yes we do have a great baby," I said, stumbling over the 'we' as I usually did. Helen considered herself Lizzie's other parent.

"We'll buy her the cutest clothes once we get to Paris," she said dreamily, handing Lizzie to me. "Lizzie and I can dress alike sometimes, the way my mother and I did. I have some pictures somewhere of the two of us in front of Buckingham Palace. My mother looked a lot like the queen. Tourists mistook her for the queen incognito. Did I ever tell you that?"

"Yes, you did," I said, "May times." I put Lizzie on her blanket on the floor between us.

"They took her picture standing next to them, waving at the camera."

Lizzie grabbed onto my big toe and started to gum it. It was probably unsanitary, but they say you've got to introduce babies to germs or they won't develop enough immunities.

"Your physics grade must have gone up," I said, "if you think you're going to Paris."

"Oh for heaven's sake, Elizabeth. Stop being idiotic. You and I both know my grades don't matter. And Jim Gibson doesn't matter either."

"What does?" I said.

"Listen," my mother said, with gravity. "All I wanted out of this second life was the love I didn't get in the first. From you, for one thing. In our other relationship from the day you were born I felt like you were someone else's baby. When you looked at me, I could tell there was no affection; I didn't matter to you."

"Whoa," I said. "You're getting it all mixed up."

"Whatever," she said. "What I'm talking about is you and your inability to care, really care for another human being. The closer the person the worse it gets. Some sort of veil goes up."

She should have been talking about herself the way she was twisting things around. I felt dizzy with it. Like she was still playing Lady Macbeth, messing with my head.

"I love Lizzie," I said, weakly.

"I'm warning you, daughter of mine, this is your last chance to have me in your life, to love me the way you should. If that feeble half-man, that creepy weasel, gets on our flight, you'll never see me again. And then you'll be even more of a frigid, lonely woman than you are now. Lizzie, notwithstanding."

FROZEN

I didn't answer. I couldn't. For a moment I even wondered if she was right about how cold I was with everybody who ever loved me, starting with her.

And then, Lizzie bit my toe as hard as she could. Even without teeth it hurt like hell.

"Shit," I said.

Mom laughed.

"I have an errand to take care of. I'll be back soon," she said. "I can't hang around waiting for you to figure out your own mind."

"Where are you going?" I called after her.

"I left something important in my locker," she said. "And, if he's there, I have to talk to Jim about my grades."

Why I didn't follow her, I'll never know.

I found out later that Jim was indeed in his office that Saturday afternoon, unluckily for him, putting last minute touches on his upcoming summer school graduation speech and actually thinking about Mom as in: "the amazing variety of courageous young women in our school—an Egyptian, an ex-homeless person, a girl battling cancer, an abuse survivor, and Helen, who's lived another whole life before."

Of course he couldn't say any of the above except for the Egyptian, so he was considering another tack when Helen blasted through his door, hammer in hand, looking something like a Russian proletarian from an old propaganda poster, except the hammer should have been a sickle and she needed a bandanna around her hair.

"Why, hello there, Helen," Jim had said. And then, because he hadn't made the transition in his sweet mind from nutty Helen to insane, cold-blooded murderer, he began to sing, "If I had a hammer."

Which is when she slammed him over the head.

He fell over sideways behind his desk, where he twitched a bit until he finally lay still. She kicked his left leg and then his rib cage experimentally. He didn't budge. Also, because blood had begun to spurt out his nose, she figured he was probably dead, leaving her the room and time to apply herself to his computer.

Remarkably, given her lack of technical prowess, she was able to change her summer school grades to a B. Then she wiped off the keyboard with a Kleenex she found on Jim's desk and ran back to her Volvo, which she'd promised to loan Nick, while we were in Paris, if he paid the registration and insurance. Mom didn't give anything away for free.

She stopped at the ice cream store on the way home and bought us a mint chocolate ice cream cake with the words "*Vive La Paris*" written in big purple script on the top.

"Yum," I said, cutting myself a big piece and taking a bite. "What a great idea to get us a celebration cake." I was hoping that's all she'd been up to.

She watched me eat, expressionless. She looked different, older, more like herself when I knew her before. It was weird. She looked like the life was draining out of her, fast.

"Don't you want some before it melts?" I said.

And then I noticed what looked like blood splatter on her t-shirt. I pointed.

"Whose blood is it this time?"

"Chocolate," she said, pulling it over her head.

"Shit, Helen, what have you done now?" I said. She sat down next to me on the couch and leaned over like she was going to faint. When her skin touched mine, I felt how cold and clammy it was.

"I don't feel good," she said.

"Stop acting," I said. "You're just all worked up about Paris. I told you we'd go."

"It's like I'm having a heart attack. I couldn't let Jim come."

"Oh my god. What have you done to him?"

She tumbled to the floor and began to shake.

"I'll get you a glass of water," I said.

Her face was turning red and tiny wrinkles were forming around her eyes and mouth.

"Help me," she whispered, sounding more like those dying babies at Stillwaters than a cute teen. But at that moment, I heard Lizzie crying from her crib down the hall.

"I'll be right back," I said.

I took my time with the baby because I still figured Mom was acting, not dying. She'd been acting all her lives, pretending to be a decent human being the last time and this time a lovely young woman who wasn't a serial killer. And always everything was my fault. I was the cold, unfeeling daughter who never cared.

The baby held out her arms and I lifted her up to me.

"Little Lizzie," I said, blowing air onto her soft stomach.

She giggled like a cartoon character, so I did it some more.

"Come help me," Mom called as loud as she could. Her voice rattled. I turned around and saw that she was crawling down the hall. It was awful.

"I'll call 9-11," I said.

After I called the dispatcher, I got her the glass of water and sat with her on the floor. After a few moments, I put her head on my lap and stroked her forehead while she groaned. She wasn't acting after all. I could see her skin getting saggy and mottled with age spots right before my eyes. Pink foam was coming out her mouth.

After the ambulance came, I called the cops and told them, anonymously, that there'd been an incident at Bentwood school in the principal's office. It wouldn't matter if I was wrong, and it might save Jim's life if I was right.

Finally I got Doreen to come over and babysit Lizzie. I didn't tell her why I had to leave because if she knew Helen was probably dying, she might want to come.

I don't know why I was so calm during Mom's crisis. Maybe the end seemed inevitable. Her second life had always been too good to last; Mom getting to come back young and beautiful, uninhibited and protected, full of hope and zest. Too good and too awful at the same time.

It was nothing worth fighting for, that was for sure. And the great thing was that if she died, soon, she wouldn't get to ruin my life or Lizzie's anymore. And that thought made me smile. I just didn't know what I was going to tell the doctors. Maybe they'd come up with some disease I didn't know about.

Once I had time to think about what Mom might have done to Jim, I wasn't so calm. While I followed her ambulance to the hospital, I called ahead to see if he'd been admitted. It made altogether too much sense that she'd try to take him out before he ruined Paris and everything else.

A few minutes later, I parked in Tow-Away and ran into intensive care, slamming open the No Admittance doors like a madwoman.

"You can't come in here," a guy shouted at me, but I kept on running anyway. It was like I could tell where Jim was by intuition or something. They were pushing Mom's body on a gurney right behind me, so we made a regular emergency procession, as if we'd been in a war.

"Elizabeth," Mom called in her old lady voice.

"Later," I shouted.

I found Jim hooked up to tubes but still alive and actually awake.

FROZEN

"What got into Helen?" he managed to say.

"You're alive," I said, taking his cold hand. "Thank god."

"She hit me with a hammer. She left me for dead."

"That was her last act of violence," I said evenly. I looked him over. They'd managed to remove most of the blood and patch him up with stitches. His face was already turning black and blue and they'd had to shave off some of the hair on his head. I felt so terrible I couldn't stand it.

"I won't press charges if you don't want me to," he said right before he fell asleep.

I burst into tears. What a good man I'd made a baby with. And he was going to be OK.

Minerva called me on my cell at that moment, and I answered. Normally in intensive care I wouldn't have picked it up, but as soon as I heard her voice, I knew I needed her right away.

"Should I bring Kendra?" she asked me.

"No, I don't want her to see Helen this way," I said. "Jim's in here too, in intensive care. She hit him over the head with a hammer."

"Jim, the principal and father of your child?"

"Yep," I said, kind of losing my voice.

"Are you crying? Hang on. I'll be there right away."

I told her to meet me in Mom's room.

They'd evidently stabilized her or given up. The doctor told me they were running tests, but that it looked like a form of Progeria, a disease of accelerated aging. Personally, I figured her wiring was burning out from all the violence, but what difference did that make?

Had I noticed any signs before this, the doctor wanted to know. Blah, blah, blah.

All I wanted to do was get myself alone with Mom so I could grill her on Jim before the lights went out.

"You did it, didn't you?" I said to her. She was sitting up in the hospital bed examining her hands, which were wrinkled with age spots. Her hair was gray.

"Ugly," she said in her old lady's voice.

It would have been sad if it hadn't been Mom.

"Answer me."

"Pardonez-moi?"

She was still practicing her French and, to me, she looked like she had half an hour left of life. When would she let go?

"You tried to kill Jim."

"Tried?" she said. "You mean he's not dead? Merde."

"He's in the hospital, all bandaged up."

Mom lay there, finally defeated. I'd never ever seen her like this. I could almost watch the last of her life force slip away. I had to lean down to hear her voice.

"He was going to take you from me. Once we got to Paris, you were going to go off with him and Lizzie. You promised to stay with me forever, and you were about to leave me, just like Daddy and Jeremy and ..." she paused to catch her breath.

"You're making that up," I said. "He's not my boyfriend. I wouldn't have left you, ever."

She wasn't listening. She was reviewing both her lives in her last few minutes.

"And my first boyfriend. He left me too."

I took her hand. She pulled it away.

"I think you're dying, Mom," I said.

"I did it for us," she said.

I couldn't take it anymore. I closed the door so I could shout at her in private.

"There is no us, Mom. There never was. It was all wishful thinking. For both of us. There aren't any second chances either. You have to accept the life you're given and then get on with it."

I pulled one of her pillows out from behind her head.

I knew she was going to die soon, but I wanted to be the one to kill her first. I held the pillow above her head for a moment, thinking about what I was about to do. The door opened before I could lower my arms.

It was Minerva, thank god.

"Let me help you, honey," she said without missing a beat.

So I took the left side of the pillow and Min took the right.

We pushed down in perfect unison and held on tight while Mom fought back. The whole time I looked into Min's brown eyes, which were filled with, what else can I call it, perfect love.

EPILOGUE

◆

Now, three years later, we were all making our way up the steep hill to Mom's grave. For good measure, I'd had her cremated. We'd buried her ashes in a lovely forested cemetery full of English chapels, rose gardens and even a giant marble memorial to veterans of war. Mom would have fully approved.

Lizzie pulled away from me as soon as she could and ran to the redwood tree that stood near the marker. She was full of energy and joy, the way kids are. Most of the time, when it was safe, I let her take off to romp like a big puppy without a care for anything except this exact moment. I half expected her to try to roll back down the hill towards us, but evidently there was something better to do at the top.

I was holding Min's hand. David and Raoul were behind us carrying, as usual, balloons. It was Mom's original birthday, and I thought it was about time we visited her ashes. Next to the boys were Jim and Doreen, holding hands too. It turned out they'd gotten to know each other when he came over to visit Lizzie and me after work. His face had taken a while to heal and Doreen knew a lot about wound care from old Mom's infections, so that's how it started, I guess.

Doreen and Jim spent a lot of time talking about wedding plans and he'd even bought her a sapphire engagement ring.

By now, everybody knew everything about Mom, except that Min and I had smothered her before her natural death occurred. That was our secret alone.

"Why'd you help me?" I'd asked her later, after she left poor Frank for the last time.

"I researched cryonics and David Emerson. It wasn't hard. Getting reanimated was exactly like something your Mom would do. I kind of figured out what was going on."

"But smothering her?"

"She ruined your life twice; anybody could see that. With her gone for good I was pretty sure you'd finally be able to let somebody close. Namely me."

"We could have waited," I said, "for her to die on her own."

"No we couldn't. We had to make sure."

Besides, using my muscles to squeeze the breath out of her released something in me, something huge. I didn't explain that part to Min, but I knew she could tell.

Right now, I gave Min a big kiss on the mouth.

"We're here," I said.

The gravestone looked beautiful. 'Helen Pruitt', it read, – 'Rest in Peace Forever.'

"This was your grandmother, Lizzie," I said, holding her still in front of me as we all looked down.

"Is she in heaven, Mommy?"

We all looked at each other.

"No honey," I said. "She's right under there, where she belongs."

CPSIA information can be obtained at www.ICGtesting.com
Printed in the USA
BVOW031837140313

315584BV00009B/130/P